THE EATER OF DARKNESS

Robert M. Coates

❧❧ ❧❧

THE EATER
OF DARKNESS

WITH AN INTRODUCTION WRITTEN
SPECIALLY FOR THIS EDITION

CAPRICORN BOOKS

G. P. PUTNAM'S SONS   NEW YORK

© 1959 G. P. PUTNAM'S SONS
Library of Congress Catalog
Card Number 59-15150

MANUFACTURED IN THE UNITED STATES OF AMERICA

To

My Father and Mother
Nick Carter
"Sapper" (H. C. McNeille)
Elsa
Kathleen Cannell
ex-Mayor Hylan
Gertrude Stein
Robert McAlmon
George Laflin Miller
Oleg Skrypitzine
J. C. Henneberger
Gerald Chapman
Harold Loeb
The New York Times
Jeannie Oliver Arnold, M.D.
I. B. F.
and
Fantômas
This book is affectionately
or gratefully dedicated.

Iunctis viribus molestum contempsimus.

PETRONIUS ARBITER.

Introduction

By ROBERT M. COATES

I WOULD be both a fool and a liar if I didn't admit straightaway that I'm delighted to see this first book of mine re-published. If the first novel is like the first-born child—and it is, for it is always regarded a little more tenderly and forgivingly than the ones that follow—then it seems to me that the same novel, re-issued, is a little like the appearance of the first grand-child. There is the same sense of being at one remove, combining the pleasures of parenthood without its pains and anxieties, and the same respectful feeling that one is involved, despite one's self, in the ancient processes of continuity; and the easy, irresponsible fondness—most of all, perhaps, the feeling of irresponsibility. "I didn't write the thing," the grandfather-author says. "If anyone's to blame, blame him," and ignoring the paradox in time he points to his spiritual son, that young-ster in his twenties, back there.

i

There is also that grandfatherly tendency to lean back and reminisce. Can you spare me a moment or two while I light my pipe? Then I'll tell you about the early and middle nineteen-twenties—or as we call them, the good old days.

To begin with, this book was written in what I am convinced were happier, more hopeful and confident times than we are likely to see again for many, many years. Every age, every generation, in its youth, has its problems, its trials, its triumphs and its uncertainties. We had ours. But apart from all this mine had also the glorious feeling that we were truly on the threshold of a Golden Age. We had it on the highest authority that the last great war, the War To End Wars, had been fought—hadn't even President Wilson said so?—and we believed it. And not only we, but a good share of our elders believed it too; I can still remember the outcries of horror and condemnation that swept the world when Laurence Stallings published that massive compilation of war photographs, around 1925, and titled it "The First World War". "First World War," indeed! There was fighting going on here and there sporadically, of course: in the Riff, against Abd El Krim, and mysterious doings in Russia; the Japanese were beginning to throw their weight around in Manchuria. But that there would ever be another Great War—*that* was unthinkable; surely we had all learned our lesson about that!

Stallings was right, of course, and already there were forces slowly gaining strength and direction which would eventually justify his ironic prediction. But I won't go into them here, for we didn't know about them. The young men of my generation looked forward to peace, to peace timeless, unhurried and indestructible; I would suggest that you pause for a moment, as I sometimes do, to think about that, and compare the basic outlook it suggests with the mixture of frustration, anxiety and downright fear that lies in the back of every man's mind nowadays when he picks up his morning paper or turns on the radio.

This fact, too, I think, had a great deal to do with creating the atmosphere of the period— a mixture of optimism, enthusiasm and feverish activity. It was a fine time to be young in, especially in Paris and for a bunch of kids from

Pittsburgh, Cincinnati, Rochester, Dallas and other way stations who until the war had hardly known Europe existed. It was the Dada period, and for me Dada has always meant gaiety: the one artistic movement I know of whose main purpose was having fun. It was also a period of experimentation. There was indeed a ferment in all the arts, and in the field of literature we had three titans leading the way—Gertrude Stein, James Joyce and Ezra Pound—who in their separate fashions were manipulating the English language in ways that had never been done before; and if the headiness of all this made us sometimes a little punch-drunk or just plain silly it must, I think, be conceded that we were honestly so.

Unlike the present "beat" generation, which sometimes seems to me to be playing both ends against the middle, we felt that if we were in revolt we could neither give quarter to the enemy nor accept it. We were so far out, as the saying goes now, that success distressed us. Our "little" magazines—Broom, Gargoyle, Secession, transition, and so on—remained determinedly little, eschewing anything so vulgar as wide circulations and financial profits; while a good review, if it came from one of the pooh-bahs of the period, was equally disturbing. Praise from such a quarter could only mean that you had slipped up somewhere, and I still remember my uneasiness when an early book of mine, "The Outlaw Years," *was* successful: what had I done, I wondered, to deserve such loathsome encomiums? (One of the French Dadaists, Louis Aragon— now, oddly enough, a leading figure in the Communist party over there, and presumably with no time for such nonsense—went so far as to write the book editors of the Paris papers individually, promising to horsewhip them if they so much as mentioned his new book. Most of us had our parents to support us, of course—or to help, as mine did, while I earned a little money on the side—and the cost of living, owing to the exchange, was almost embarrassingly low. My average income, from all sources, was about fifty dollars a month, and I certainly never felt deprived.)

This book, though it wasn't an actual flop, had a gratifying lack of success in the proper quarters, and a pleasantly comforting succès d'estime elsewhere. The fact is that I'd honestly never expected to see it published in the first place, so in a sense anything I got out of it was gravy. My attitude at the time was a confused, variable and thoroughly jejune mixture of François Villon (the medieval influence and also general rascality, though a more law-abiding rascal than I was in those days could hardly be imagined); Sir Philip Sidney (the great sixteenth-century English poet, representing the aristocratic impulse) and Dada, or devil-may-careness. In this instance, it was largely Sidney's influence that governed me.

Like many of his high-born contemporaries, he never stooped to seek out a publisher for his writings. He just had a fair copy of them made and circulated it among his friends, and I figured that if that was the way Sidney did things, why, so would I. I was back in New York for a year, trying to recoup, or perhaps simply coup my finances (after all, I couldn't depend on my family forever) when the early part of the book was written. But I finished it in Giverny, a lovely small Seine-side town about fifty miles down the river from Paris—having managed, more or less by the skin of my teeth, to get back to France again—and Giverny, though fundamentally a farm village, and a charming one, had been a resort for artists and writers ever since Claude Monet had settled there some fifty years earlier.

He was still living there, the patriarch of the place, as he was of the whole Impressionist movement; and so, by that time, was a grandson, another artist, half French and half American, named James Butler. Jim was also a dabbler in all sorts of handicrafts, and the purpose of this long digression, nostalgic as it is to me, is to say that when the book was finished I simply typed it off carefully, and with Jim's help managed to bind it fairly neatly—and thought that would be the end of it. Or not quite the end, for there still remained the gentlemanly circularization of friends; and one of the friends, and a particularly dear one, whom I tapped in this manner, was Gertrude Stein. She read it, and liked it, and immediately set about getting it published. Though I may have yawned delicately at the prospect, I must admit now that I was pretty darned pleased at the way things were turning out. I can see now that a good deal of my disdain at the idea of mingling art with commerce, like a good many of our other attitudes of the period, was basically simply hedging: I wasn't at all sure that anybody was going to want to publish the thing in the first place.

I have my reservations about parts of the book now, but have made relatively few changes. I have changed or tried to clarify a few references that were so personal or so much of the period that they'd be needlessly cryptic now, but otherwise I have made no effort to "bring it up to date." There *were* Elevateds in New York then, and they did cost a nickel a ride; there was vaudeville, and the movies were silent and had captions; girls (God bless them) did wear a chemise; and Giverny (God bless it too) though now almost a suburb of Paris, was then so quietly rural at night that you *could* hear the old water mill on the river nearby throbbing "so soft it might be thunder in Constantinople."

I have tampered with a couple of passages that really grieved me, but I've left others that are equally improvable if they seemed to require more ambitious changes. Though it's probably the most "personal" of all, I've left the voluminous dedication as is, for sentimental reasons. It was intended, in a kind of grab-bag way, as a tribute to friends and other persons or organizations who had helped in one way or another in the book's production. Robert McAlmon, for instance, who was getting out Contact Editions in Paris, at considerable cost to his own writing, was the book's first publisher; Nick Carter, "Sapper" and Fantômas, their French equivalent, were among the writers of thrillers on whom the book was modeled; the New York Times comes on the list because its Sunday magazine section was a welcome customer for the "color" stories I wrote (odd corners of New York, even odder corners of Paris, and so on) which helped finance it, and Gerald Chapman was a bank robber and gunman very much in the news at the time . . . perhaps that's enough to give the general idea.

As I've said, Gertrude Stein, who is also mentioned in the dedication, was the one who practically *got* the book published; but she was a help, a support and an encourager in ways that went quite beyond that. One wonderful thing about the nineteen-twenties in Paris, as I look back on them, was that the "great ones," even the titans, were so accessible. You didn't have to make an appointment, and a pilgrimage, to meet Leger, Picasso, Satie, Pascin, Juan Gris, Tristan Tzara or Brancusi, to mentioned a few names at random. You found them sitting at a table nearby on the terrasse of the Café du Dome, the Select or the Rôtonde, in the Montparnasse Quarter, or the Deux Magôts in the Saint-Germain, and as the evening wore on and mutual friends appeared you were likely to find yourself sitting at the same table with them, or at their table infinitely rounded out, satellited, with other tables—and talking and drinking with them without the least self-consciousness on either side.

Brancusi was a great party-giver and so in those days was Pound, and at both their houses there was the same feeling of equality between the older and more established artists and the young newcomers. In a sense, the atmosphere has always seemed to me a little like that of the

Cripple Creek gold-mining district, where I lived
for a while as a boy: with everyone striving for
new strikes or new discoveries, anyone might
strike it rich, and meanwhile there was room
for all.

James Joyce was an exception, being more re-
tiring, and so was Gertrude Stein, who just didn't
like the randomness of cafe life. A big woman,
calm, massive-faced, massive-bodied, with a
brown Italian coloring that was accentuated by
her habit of wearing loose-woven peasant-like
skirts and blouses, and sandals, she lived with her
life-long friend, Alice Toklas (darker, wirier
and more active) in the famous apartment,
27 rue de Fleurus, off the Luxembourg Gardens,
and in a sense presided there. I think now that
she may have felt a certain frustration herself,
for in her lifetime she never got (has not got
even now) the recognition that was due her for
her influence in introducing an almost mathematical lucidity (the classic influence, as distinguished from Joyce's, the romantic influence)
into the treatment of the English language.

At any rate, people came to her, not she to

them—Sherwood Anderson, Thornton Wilder, Ernest Hemingway, among many others—and though a few of them, notably Hemingway, disavowed her later, I think most of us remember and treasure the warmth, the understanding and (again) the feeling of artistic equality we got from her.

I won't go further into that, though, for I feel I'm in danger of getting soppy, and I've certainly talked enough about myself. Instead, I'd like to use the space remaining to me to add one more anecdote to the annals of Steiniana. I'll make it as brief as possible. We'd got talking one day about Anthony Trollope, who was one of her great admirations, and when I confessed I'd never read him she promised casually to send me some books of his. A few days later an expressman delivered, not a parcel, but a carton, a crate full, heavy with books—with Trollope, in short: the Barchester series, the Parliamentary series, practically all of him, and as you probably know all of Trollope means a great deal of reading indeed.

I was wading in Trollope for months, I was practically drunk with him, for I discovered that

I loved him too. But I still feel that if you're going to get to know Trollope, that's the way to do it, and the way Gertrude handled the matter is typical of the largeness of her own nature, too.

1959

CONTENTS

THE EATER OF DARKNESS

APOLOGUE

IT seems it had been years but (she was remembering: a cold gray wind and the leaves went stuttering along the walls of the rue Clovis) it was hard keeping the cobblestones silent as into the rue Descartes; a man (waving a green pantaloon before the autobus) flattening into arm in arm.

"Et après ça Madame?" (reëchoing).

"Après ça il me faut une livre de carottes." (She fed herself into the vast conveyorbelt of plate-glass windows blue signs with gold letters is the Place de la Contrescarpe (the expectant autobusses rustling with hooded plumage in the trees) and he had said)

"You must come and see me sometime": he had said:

"Will you come and see me sometime I will show you my studio the address is we will make tea together I shall give you tea": he had said:

"Come. You must come as to tea no matter but I shall cover you with the fragile petals of muguets and cigarette ashes so that your nudity may be scented and terrestrial by these means I shall drag you down from the stars placing violets on the nipples of your breasts roses and green vines in the (oh! kiss-fertile) hollows of your knees I shall bring you within the compass of my arms": he had said and mentioning the number.

After that it had been easy and (she remembering) the rue Lacepède the rue (feeling smotheringly the smooth slipping of silk along the cool flesh of her thighs) Gracieuse the rue du Puits-de-l'Ermite (remembering) walking:

❖

The concierge had had white hairy eyes very much like a photograph fading spottingly in the 1890 manner or still more closely resembling one of those wild thin figures seen walking after midnight above the Subway gratings on Seventh Avenue, and wielding her meager face like a broom:

"No. Monsieur Charles is not here any more."

(And (dropping like a penny in the slot machine French Girls Delight) between two men at the curbstone: she remembering)

"When will he be back?"

"God knows. He has gone to America."

The words tolled like a deathknell in her ear. Steadying herself with one hand against a large terracotta flowerpot which ornamented the square pillar at the foot of the stairs:

"Did he leave no word no address no message for me?"

"No," said the concierge. "You can," she added, intermittently rubbing a dustcloth against the face of a tall walnut clock, "go up and see if you desire. The studio is for rent."

She remembering opening the door and all floating glittering against the dusty air now:

(1) the tapestry from Yucatan it had hung over the fireplace,

(7) the tin garbage can in which he had kept his clay near the window,

(4) the square of Chinese silk; the (3) walnut table,

(5) the strip of muslin printed with marching kings she had once worn it as a sash dancing for him in a moment of abandon,

(6) the empty parrot's cage they had decorated it with watercolors together:

Tenantless days and the place was already haggard in rigor mortis: it needed sweeping: he had not even left the empty parrot's cage they had decorated in watercolors for her. Descending again to the concierge:

"I will take the studio. How much is it by the month?" she had said.

"Three hundred and fifty francs," said the concierge.

◆

She was (she was remembering) walking:

I—MONITORY FIGURES

WE next find him in a rooming house. This rooming house was located on West Twenty-Third Street,[1] New York City, near the point where the street, changing from its air of frontier respectability, breaks into a slouching run for the Hoboken Ferry. The rooming house had a smooth brown front and brown worn steps which leaped into the entrance door like a rabbit into its hole. The house shivered clammily about you as you entered.

In the window nearest the doorway on the groundfloor was a small brass sign indicating the existence of the Seaside Employment Agency.

From the hallway, however, a door gave into what had anciently been the parlor of the house when it had been occupied by a doctor, or more

[1] For reasons obvious to anyone familiar with the course of diplomatic events during the last half century, the street number cannot be revealed at this time.

probably by one of those families of the Eighties whose only outward show of life was when at ten sharp of every Sunday morning three ladies in bloomer-sleeved and wideskirted frocks descended the steps accompanied by a tall gentleman in frock coat and white gloves on their way to attend divine service at the Seventh Baptist Church. In this room, or parlor, the now chief ornaments were six highly glazed china canaries, arranged meticulously on the mantel of a pink marble non-practicable fireplace.

And since one, on inquiring for rooms, was ushered into this room, and since, sitting on one of the goldleaf chairs, one saw through the stiff lace curtains the blank back of the little brass sign heretofore alluded to, the exact location of the Seaside Employment Agency became, in the woolly moments of waiting for the entrance of the landlady, a matter for the keenest conjecture.

In fact the problem, and the possibilities of its solution attendant on such an act, were among the deciding factors moving Charles Dograr to engage a room there.

Two months and three days, however, had

passed. He had progressed no whit nearer the solution of the mystery.

In the meantime, Charles Dograr lived in a little room on the top floor.

The room consisted of an aisle bluecarpeted between the bed and the wall of the next room which in all probability was similarly arranged and so across the front of the house. At the foot of the bed, this aisle was barricaded by a bureau or chest of drawers. Early in his occupancy, Charles Dograr had pushed this bureau or chest of drawers aside, so that he might get to his window with the view of opening it at night and closing it in the morning.

There was also a chair.

From the window, one could look across the street, where a lady on the third floor had rigged a rope along the framework of the fire escape, on which she hung pink silk chemises alternately with blue.

Charles Dograr was quite content in his modest quarters.

In this room, then, for two months and four days, he had subsisted on graham crackers and

a box of powdered milk, which he had bought
in a delicatessen on Seventh Avenue as a reward
to himself for having discovered that its name,
when read backward, spelled 'milK.'

At three o'clock every afternoon, he read a
chapter in Macaulay's "History of the English
Nation." Often he lay abed all day, with his
hands clasped beneath his chin on the pillow,
while the chambermaid would come to the door
and gaze at him bewilderedly.

He had only seven dollars in cash, and eighteen
francs ninety centimes wrapped in a handkerchief. No one had told him about the want ads
in the daily papers so he had no idea of how one
went about getting a job.

Occasionally, also, he looked through the pages
of a by now wellthumbed copy of the *Cosmo-
politan Magazine* he had picked up in Madison
Square and speculated on the impregnability of
the morals of the young actresses whose photographs were printed in the rotogravure section.
Daily, upon rising, he thanked God heartily for
having preserved him from the perils of his trans-
atlantic voyage, and for His solicitous watch-

fulness during the first few days of residence in a strange land among strange people, whose ways were foreign to him.

But he enjoyed walking along Lexington Avenue, and from the fact that all the shopwindows along Broadway were brightly lighted, even though his promenades extended well past the hour of midnight, he drew a pleasurable thrill of fear.

Moreover, when the evenings bored him, he occupied himself with cutting out bits of paper into intricate designs. So, on the whole, he was quite happy, though a little apprehensive of the future.

II—THE X-RAY BULLET

O NE night, however, he was returning at five A. M. and his breast burdened with a longing for human companionship. The stairs mounting wearily ahead of him he paused at the third landing. A crack of light beneath a door had caught his eye and thinking to rest himself with a half hour of conversation he pushed open the door and walked in.

"Well, well, well, well, well, well, well," said the old gentleman as if he had been expecting him. "Sit in that chair."

Charles Dograr did as he had been directed. The old gentleman turned back to the table, or desk with marble top, at which he had been working. Charles Dograr observed that he had a remarkably white brow and long sinuous hands. He was naked, except that he wore a pair of long green silk stockings. His back was covered by a mass of tattooed inscriptions arranged in orderly rows and interspersed with formulæ and geometric designs like a page from a mathematical textbook.

Apparently these had bearing on the work in which he was engaged, for occasionally he would pause among his siphons, bunsen burners, retorts, hydrometers, test-tubes, vernier scales, microscopes, aerometers, transformers, dynamometers, induction coils, crucibles to (with the aid of two small carved ivory handmirrors which he kept constantly at hand on the table before him) transcribe some one among the mass of notations and formulæ on his back.

The room was suffocated with the light from four hydrogen lamps in sockets on the ceiling. Over the head of the old gentleman Charles Dograr (thinking it at first an ocular illusion due to the superabundance of illumination) noticed a glittering sheet of light, curving umbrella-like downward as if some plane, otherwise invisible, refracted the rays of the powerful electrics. The room was still.

At the old gentleman's right, on the table, a

black cloth shrouded some large and apparently intricate apparatus or machine.

Once, as he worked, the old gentleman pointed with a snakelike finger at his left leg.

"Table of logarithms," he said.

Charles Dograr cleared his throat. "Really?" he commented with vague politeness. "I live on the floor above, in the little—"

The old gentleman waved his hand impatiently. "Sh-h-h! Sh-h-h!" he whispered emphatically. "It's not yet time."

"I thought—" continued Charles Dograr, like a stone rolling downhill.

"Never mind," replied the old gentleman. "Wait!"

He was heating a test-tube over the flame. The liquid clouded, changed color, was green. The old gentleman chuckled. Someone snored in an adjoining room. Charles Dograr felt his mind slipping out of his body like a hand out of a glove. A pungent aroma invaded the air. The lights were hot. The old gentleman was pouring the contents of the test-tube into an orifice of the machine under the black cloth. He was tampering shrewdly with the lever of a stop valve as he did so, and watching the needle of a dial. He had lifted a corner of the black cloth, disclosing a spiderweb antenna strung between two blue-glass-rimmed apertures at the rear of a porcelain box and was busying himself with some thumb-screw adjustments.

Charles Dograr was lying back in his chair; his mind dazedly wandering; his nose, in the muskflavored air, the peaked roof of his soul.

How long he lay there he did not know. The night had been throbbing silently about him. Suddenly it was as if the room had been jerked up and down twice or thrice, but with such in-finite rapidity that the motion had been imper-ceptible, save that a thrilled commotion re-mained in the air, leaving the room pulsing. He saw that the old gentleman had reached under the table and had pulled a lever.

The cloth had been stripped from the ma-chine. It consisted of cogs, cams, levers, wires, coils, springs watchlike in delicacy converging in a tube, blued like a rifle barrel but not more than 2½ inches long and slightly flaring at the mouth.

This tube was mounted on a swivel-joint controlled by a thumbscrew, making it susceptible of movement through an arc of approximately 135 degrees, and its movement was registered on a dial set in the base of the machine, where also a compass and incidence-meters made it possible accurately to orient the aim of the barrel. In general, the apparatus looked like a stereopticon gone berserk with machinery. Charles Dograr saw the ends of two electrodes, heavily insulated, in the box-like roof of the (as it appeared to be) incandescent-chamber. There were two other connections, sunk deep in Schiss-Mayer sockets, at the side of the contrivance. A jackknife switch lay open between them.

"Come now," said the old gentleman, as he folded the black cloth away. And, as Charles Dograr lay a moment, collecting his faculties, "Come on! It's ready."

Charles Dograr walked toward him. Midway through the room, he stumbled against something. Before he could regain his balance, he had swayed forward flinging out his hands, and had fallen heavily against a smooth, almost perpendicular surface, cold to the touch, *invisible* to the eye, which barred him off from the old gentleman whose bright eyes were watching him amusedly!

"That's my own invention!" he cried proudly, "The Dead Plane!"

Charles remained a moment, his spine prickly. He saw his hands, sustaining him against nothingness, saw the flesh at the side of his palms flattened under his weight against the chill invisible substance!

There was a crackling flare. The obstruction had been withdrawn. Considerably shaken, but oddly unafraid, he walked over to the side of the old gentleman.

The old gentleman looked at him slyly but cheerily. Within the Dead Plane, as the old gentleman had called it, the air was dull, and still. The earth is a great sleeper, and the heave of its deep-vaulted, slumbering belly sets everything on its surface to rocking in a rhythm so innate in us that we never, perhaps, perceive it. Suffice it to say that not until he had stepped inside the Dead Plane did Charles Dograr, looking at the chair on which the old gentleman sat, at the table, at the machine upon it, understand fully the meaning of the term, "inanimate object."

These were still, motionless—but, gazing back through the microscope-slide phosphorescence of the Plane at the room he had just left, he saw (was it the shifted veiling of the Plane? was it that here, from this suspended hub of silence, he saw the tremulous, eternal pulse of Life itself?) the furniture, the walls, the chair on which he had been sitting rippled over with the beat of an inward pulsation, vibrating like objects seen in a mirage.

As he stared, the Dead Plane glowed gradually visible, like a mist of ice, or rather as if a dense fog had been shaved in parabolic slices by a larger contrivance than those with which ham is cut in butcher shops. The outer room was vanishing behind an opalescent, translucent haze.

"I can close it down completely," chirped the old gentleman.

He moved a lever farther. A humming that had been faint became insistent. The Dead Plane clouded utterly, dense white opaque. The outer room was shut away. They were alone together in their cupola of silence, their faces glazed by the gray light of the interior of a submarine.

"Sit there. No. Put your eye to the left ocula-scope. That's right."

Rising V-shaped from a hooded housing at the base of the blue light-barrel were two tubes, ending each in an eyepiece lensed like the instru-ments of an optometrist. Charles Dograr seated himself at the left of the machine, his eye to one lens. The old gentleman, he observed, had taken his place at the other, and his hand grasped a lever.

"Look!"

He saw nothing. The eye of the lens stared at blackness. And then (in the corner of his eye he saw the hand move on the lever) it was as if he stared down the path of a searchlight, focuss-ing an inch-wide disk of light on the clouded surface of the Plane.

It was an instant only. Then the disk had cut like an auger through the Plane, and the tiny circle of vision centred in blackness lay against the wall of the room. He saw a fragment of picture frame, a segment of wallpaper design.

Rodlike again it leaped beyond, his eye following. It touched the arm of a sleeper in the room beyond the wall—bedclothes—a giltbrass knob at the foot of the iron bedstead . . . it pierced the other wall—was boring the night-clad street—lay against the bricks of the house across the way . . . he saw blurringly. . . .

"Keep the focus. There, beside your eye-aperture."

He found the collar-swivel adjustment (as on field glasses) and the disk of sight leaped into clarity again. The old gentleman was increasing (by means of his lever) the (or what appeared to be, for Charles Dograr saw a pointer advance along a scale reading:

Yds. . . 10 . . 20 . . 30 . . (up to) . . 5000 beside the lever slot) focus or range of the contrivance.

Then he glued his eye to the aperture again.

Successively (as the range increased) he followed the x-ray bullet through the wall of the

opposite house—a chandelier—plaster ceiling—
beams—rafters. . . .

It impinged on the left nipple of the lady
across the street, passed slantingly through the
tissues, nerves, veins, arteries, bones of her body,
issuing at a point slightly below the small of her
back, whence (more rapidly as the old gentleman more eagerly extended the focus) it progressed swiftly through:

a bottle of glue
three eggs in a windowbox
a cigar
the mechanism of an alarm clock
the chain of an electric light fixture
four pages of the Daily News
the hand of the reader
an orange
an El station turnstile
a goldfish bowl
a cushion
the calf of a woman's leg
two kissing lips
an iron handrail

a corset string
a garbage can
a plate of ham sandwiches
Laurence Vail
Peggy Guggenheim
a pack of cards
a glass eye
two felt slippers
the C in a Chop Suey sign
a cigarette holder
an umbrella
Reginald Marsh
a bottle of gin
an art-bronze book-rack
Theodore Dreiser
a clogged drain pipe
a sheaf of Shulte Cigar Store coupons
H. L. Mencken
a stiletto
Kenneth Burke
a stethoscope
a Martini cocktail
two pretzels
a cocktail shaker

Julian Levi
Arthur Moss
a pack of Luckies
Skeat's Etymological Dictionary
a copy of the New Yorker
a filing cabinet
seven picture post cards
a hot water bottle
a string of sausages
the handle of a frying pan
several bananas
an aspirin
a bottle of Zonite
a young girl
a pair of bedroom slippers
three shirts in a laundry bag
a bottle of ink
a dog's tail
a two-cent stamp
Mona Raille
a pajama button
the teeth of a man yawning
the left fender of a truck
a copy of True Confessions

a cup of coffee
a marble-topped table
a red necktie
a cross-town car
a taxicab
the tassel on a lady's garter
Malcolm Cowley
a tree
a street lamp in an open park. . . .

"I call myself the 'Eater of Darkness,'" the old gentleman chuckled. The pointer was at 2250 yds. The x-ray rod of light had now launched on a long flight through darkness, save where once it flashed on and through the spars of a ship its pennant waving. They were traversing the Hudson.

"Look inside," commanded the old gentleman, opening a pinhole slot in the side of the machine. Charles looked—once—and drew back affrighted. He had never conceived such an inferno of cold incandescence. There had been no glare—if anything only a pale colorless glow.

But it was as if a splinter of the sun had pierced his retina.

"I'll see if I can screw her up to 3000. She ought to stand it tonight."

Charles felt the old gentleman's hand crawling crablike along his leg as the lever advanced and the x-ray bullet bored on.

> a pillar of the porch of a Colonial house
> a brass doorknob
> a hall stand
> red velvet curtains
> the transverse of a dim room
> a Morris chair
> a man's knee. . . .

"Ah! We've got something at last!"

The disk swung upward. A man's back—his vest button—a cigar—the nose—the socket of an eye. . . .

Two inches more, and Charles Dograr gazed at the inner vaultings of a living skull, at the dark and convoluted interior of the brain of that distant man!

The old gentleman leaned back and stared at

Charles Dograr. Charles Dograr looked at the old gentleman and within his heart, he not knowing why nor whence it came, a sense of bitter and destructive mirth had seated itself and sat rocking his body with silent laughter.

"Let's read that," said the old gentleman. A moment later he dictated: "2,976 yards and about 2 feet." Charles noted down the figures.

"And now—see that switch?—between the two connections? Here are rubber gloves. When I say: 'Now!'—CLOSE THE SWITCH!"

Their eyes went back to the oculascopes. A moment of fumbling, as the old gentleman adjusted the range. Then—

"Now!" cried the old gentleman. "Now! NOW!" in a voice like a mortar grinding pebbles.

Charles Dograr closed the switch.

Visibly, it was as if a snake of fire had wriggled out from the hooded orifice of the machine. Swift beyond sight, it had run down the thin and unswerving cylinder that marked the path of the x-ray bullet. The man's head—the brain Charles Dograr watched—jerked backward, as

if the snake had struck . . . it trembled a little
. . . then fell slowly sidewise out of the disk of
Charles' vision.

The old gentleman, unconcernedly, began to
reverse the focus.

"I'm tired of practising on flies," he remarked.

Charles Dograr's breast deflated on his terror
as on a ball of iron. One by one, the objects
through which their gaze had passed reappeared
for a moment (as the x-ray eye of the machine
retravelled its path) then vanished irretrievably
in the night.

Charles (at last even the aperture in the Dead
Plane closed; the x-ray bullet had re-entered its
hooded home; they were alone in the cupped
opacity of the Plane) watched dizzily. He knew
what he had seen.

The old gentleman was consulting the compass.
"West northwest by north, seven points," he
read. Charles' hand moved lifelessly to his pencil
and wrote it on the pad.

Now a set of maps appeared. One, labelled
'West Section,' the old gentleman quickly ori-
ented. With calipers and rule he laid out the

("Read me that distance again."—"2976 yards and about two—" "All right, that's enough") course the x-ray bullet had travelled, marked where the serpent flash of lightning had struck, looked up smiling at Charles, whose eyes were shrunk fish-skins over his horrified soul.

But the old gentleman seemed to notice naught amiss in his young disciple's behavior; he was, in fact, cheerful rather than otherwise, to all seeming. "As I say," he began without preamble, "I've quit practising on flies and such things. It is neither conclusive scientifically nor satisfactory personally. You're lucky, young man, that I brought you in here tonight. What did you think of it? You're calm enough. Good mettle underneath, I warrant that."

He had been talking at random, though his eye and manner were those of a man pursuing a hairthread point of logic. Now he suddenly produced a bottle and two tumblers, pouring a stinger for each glass. "Drink this. You can't be as steady as you look."

"No," said Charles, finding his voice suddenly weak as he spoke, "I . . . I'm not."

"Don't wonder," replied the old gentleman enthusiastically, as if the sudden collapse of Charles had been an unexpected admission of his contentions. "Struck you odd, eh? Reach out wherever we want, through darkness, bricks, wood, stone, metal, flesh—and then light a little invisible lamp at the end of our focus. Odd, eh? 'd I tell you? I call myself the Eater of Darkness. Good name. Call me that. You may not believe it, but the hardest job was to get the light-disk to cut darkness, and keep focus. Dust does it. Dust in the air. That's why I work at night, y'know. Too easy by day." A greasy leer was sliding like oil across his face. Charles felt the man's eyes move downward like fire, enveloping his body.

He felt he must speak. His words staggered.

"I called it the x-ray bullet," he ejaculated.

"X-ray bullet," the old gentleman repeated. "Good! Takes it all in." His hand pinched Charles' knee. "Clever. Clever lad. I like you."

"I can't get out of here," said Charles involuntarily, remembering the Dead Plane.

"No," said the old gentleman. There was a moment when the gaze of each settled immovably in the purpose of the other. Then the old gentleman turned to the bottle.

"Here," he suggested, "You'll need another shot before you go."

They drank together. Without glancing behind him, Charles knew that the Dead Plane had been withdrawn. He set down his glass.

"Now," he said, "I must go."

"Wait," said the old gentleman, then paused irresolute. Charles saw his thoughts flying like bats behind the old grinning face. "You'll need money," he brought out at last. Throwing open a drawer in the desk (or table) he pulled out a wad of bills and thrust it into Charles Dograr's hand. It did not seem odd to him to accept it.

"And now," concluded the old gentleman, "Watch the papers tomorrow for the account of what happened at 5:45 A. M. on Hillcrest Terrace, Union Hill. You and I know. But I want to see what the police will make of it. Drop in for dinner tomorrow together. I'll show you where to get the finest *cotelette à la bretonne* on this side of the water. We'll do a little more"—he chuckled horribly—"experimenting afterward!"

III—"EXTRA! EXTRA!"

H E went to his room for a little while, and lay sleepless on his bed. Out of the darkness, like the face of a drowned man out of the sea, the house across the street was rising pale and expressionless.

It was near dawn.

The blanket crawled over him like a caterpillar.

He got up and went for a walk.

As the front door closed blackly behind him, a door opened simultaneously across the way, in the house where the lady lived. A blonde man carrying a derby hat issued therefrom and Charles Dograr, glancing up through the bars of the fire escape that had refracted so many of his ardent glances, thought he saw a white arm waved downward from the window.

The blonde man, however, did not look back. He walked off toward Tenth Avenue, carrying his derby in his hand like a man about to empty a cuspidor.

Charles moved in the opposite direction. There was a buttery tinge along the eastern sky. The streets were gray, the pavements relentlessly deserted. In the knife-edged early light the concrete sidewalk was like a skin stretched across the drumhead of Infinity. A too-loud step might provoke a premature alarm. Charles walked gingerly, like an incognito Paul Revere.

At Ninth Avenue the floating El dangled its spiderlegs around him at Eighth Avenue a newspaper delivery truck spun past a man walked out of an allnight lunch at Seventh Avenue the houses were red along the dry street like shreds of meat on a bone at Sixth Avenue he turned north because there was a novelty store with gimcracks in its window and especially art photos of beautiful girls legally nude that he liked to look at.

Soon the first early groups of workers were moving in clumps along the sidewalk. He looked at their brutish faces and it gave him a sense, almost feminine, of fear.

There were so few of them.

For Charles Dograr was one of those rare souls whose spirit seems to have been compounded, as it were, of more fragile substance, of emotion more volatile, perception more finely tunable than the rest, so that he rode currents of intuition that others sank through seeking the rock-bottom of logic, and was uplifted and exalted by the transcendental vapors of a perhaps earthy—even, to continue the figure ad locandum, miry—concept into which others, trudging, stuck bogged and bemisted.

So sound moved him more than hearing, vision more than sight, and his instinct sucked Truth, like honey, from the flower of Life, disdaining the syllogistic distillation of the comb. Briefly, he listened to the melody, not the words, of the Eternal Song, and he was just the person—perhaps the only one alive—to imagine there was any discoverable meaning in such a passage as this, when he found it in a book.

Thus he strode along, keeping as bold a front as he might, but inwardly wondering why one of these hawkeyed Italians did not knife him, or one of these thincheeked Jews garotte him with stiff brown fingers, or one of these thickjawed Bulgars bludgeon him—all for his pockets' contents as he walked alone among them (and they so few) between the empty-glass houses.

And one man followed him! It was a dirtyish little fellow, his clothes frizzled like a cocoon and a dusty derby hat. Charles turned down Twenty-Ninth Street. Iron shutters had been rolled down, closing the driveways of the warehouses. Overhead the sky had grown dark and thunderous.

"He's a head shorter than I," thought Charles. But Fear told him that little men could kill. Napoleon, Cyrus, Cæsar whirled through his head —all little men, but indomitable. . . . He pictured the man behind him—and his steps were gaining; they were like thunder in the narrow way—he saw him a grayclad miniature thunderbolt, gritting his teeth, the hands clenched, the whole strung body tightening for the flashing destructive moment toward which it had been framed. "He will leap," thought Charles chokingly,—"from behind."

And he walked slowly, almost tottering—what did it matter? one step more or less away from his doom—and his hand slid falteringly along the slipping granite of the crowding buildings. "My money," thought Charles, "—the old gentleman; I have more than sixty dollars. . . ." And (vicariously) almost comforted—"What will he do with it? Sixty dollars. . . . Go to Chicago . . . drink . . . with sixty dollars . . ."

And then—the short sharp stab of revulsion. He sees his body lying there, lying in the gutter. Horses stumble over it. The expressman leaping down from his seat. "Good God!" And the stenographers gathering round—screaming affectedly, for what is a dead body lying there in the gutter to them? They roll him over . . . "Stabbed!"

His heart sickened. A cold miasmal fluid rose within him, choking. Here he would wait. He would turn, bravely . . . meet death. And, pivotting funereally, he turned.

With a curious crouching carriage, the little man walked fuzzily past Charles and continued down Twenty-Ninth Street.

For a moment, Charles leaned unsteadily against a hydrant, staring, dumbfounded. Twenty or thirty paces farther on, the man came to a halt, fumbling in one of the pockets of his coat. Finally he produced a key, turned the lock of a door.

With a leap Charles was upon him. He touched the man's shoulder. The thin face turned blankly, inquiringly up at him.

"What is your name?" he asked.

"Why, Rupert Pragman—Rupert C.—" began the little man in a voice like eating Grape Nuts. "Why?"

Charles felt that he could take him in his arms and weep with him. But he remained calm. There was a moment of silence.

"Is that all?" asked the little man, meekly, and began to sidle unobtrusively toward the door. Suddenly he stopped. "It isn't my wife?" he demanded, coming back with a little pounce to seize Charles' coat sleeve. *"It isn't my wife?"*

Charles shook him off. This was an untoward question; it upset him. "Do you love your wife?"

"Do I love . . . ? . . . Sure I . . . Say,

what is it to you anyway? Who are you anyway?" He tried to put on a bold face but the
eyes were like a child playing soldier. "Hey
Charlie!" he shrieked suddenly toward the interior of the vacant building. "Don't think I'm
alone here, you. What do you want anyway?"
No Charlie came.

"I'm Charlie. Charles Dograr is my name."

Abruptly, the little man tried to manœuvre
himself inside the door. Charles seized him,
dragged him back. The man gave a half-choked
squawk. Charles, until now, had preserved some
semblance of calm. But at this, the floodgates
burst.

"What's the matter with you anyway?" he
cried, as disgust ripened into wrath. "Why didn't
you kill me? You had me alone. I was waiting
. . . counting every step. And not a soul around.
Not one!" He dragged the fellow out of the
doorway, twisted his head around. "Look! Look
up the street—the other way too—not a soul in
sight. Why didn't you? Why didn't you? Do you
think I haven't got money? Why didn't you kill
me?" He cuffed him about the head, slapping his

face with the broad palm, raining questions like a schoolmaster on an offending pupil.

And—"*Good* Lord! *Good* Lord!" the little man was moaning breathless to himself struggling.

And Charles was near tears. "You . . . if you had the heart of a man . . . for your wife . . . with me all alone. . . . Listen!" He pulled him suddenly erect. "You say you love your wife. What would you do with sixty dollars?" The little man squirmed, voiceless.

Charles persisted. "What would you do? I've got it. You'd have it if you'd had guts enough. What would you do with it? Speak!"

"*Good* Lord!" cried the little man.

"Speak!"

"I—I don't know. . . . *Good Lord!*" Charles had wrenched his arm judiciously.

"How long do you have to work here for sixty dollars?" He had to crack him on the jaw before the fellow could answer.

"Two—two weeks."

"Two weeks! And in two minutes you'd have had it. What am I to you? Why shouldn't you kill me?" Charles' voice rose suddenly, jangled off human key. "God, man! Can't you speak? Can't you think? Faugh!" With a revulsion abrupt and brutal, he threw the man away from him. It was a reptile, a toad, a slimy thing to cover the hand that touched it with green scum. His hands would be foul for days. The little man scurried inside his glass door, locked it and remained inside, staring.

Charles walked to the curbstone and sat down and wept. "Humanity! Humanity!" he cried. "What is humanity that I should love it? . . . or fear it? . . . or pity it? . . . or—" this came more slowly "—hate it?"

That was judicial. "—Hate it. . . ." He turned. The little man, nose pressed to glass, gave a backward start but Charles smiled, as reassuringly as he might. Enunciating carefully, that the words might be seen though the door barred their sound, he said, "I forgive you," repeated it three times, smiled at the end, and walked away to the Pennsylvania station.

The morning papers were out, and he bought

the *American*, the *World* and the *Tribune*, then went to the benches of the waiting room.

BOMB SLAYS TEN AS
THOUSANDS STARE

But this was in Roanoke, Va.

"I KILLED HIM," SOBS SON
CONFESSING DOUBLE CRIME

—obviously not that. Nor:

BRIDE SEES HUSBAND'S
FATAL PLUNGE

though for a moment he had high hopes. But it had happened in Arcana, Ore. Hastily he turned to the second page, the third, the fourth. He found himself muttering, "Hillcrest Terrace. . . . Hillcrest Terrace, Union Hill. . . ." and checked himself sharply, glancing up to see if he had been observed. It was by such slips as this that the cleverest criminals were caught. From cover to cover of them all he went; there was no mention of his murder, so far.

"I'll wait for the evening papers," he decided

and lay back comfortably a moment, lazily watching the tide of commuters, dozen by dozen, as they rushed pell-mell for the Subway.

They had a practised way, he observed, of dropping two cents and snatching a paper at the Union News stand as they passed. "Poor devils," he thought, "Too bad it isn't in the morning papers. Give them something to read."

◈

And again—he was sitting in a quick-lunch, eating prunes and a doughnut at the counter —it came to him suddenly: "I am a murderer!"

"I am a murderer!" For a moment it seemed he had spoken it; for a moment he seemed to hear the echo of his voice rebounding from the tiled walls and he looked curiously at his neighbors—the man in brown the two sailors the man with the little black valise the truckman the plumber—eating silently. No one moved. The cashier sat behind his counter, face bent over the morning paper.

Perhaps one of these was a murderer as well. Perhaps the cashier had strangled his three-year-old daughter last night as the city lay sleeping. He had a face that curled round his blue eye like a fist around a marble. "He looks more like a murderer than I."

Charles Dograr hastily finished his doughnut. "This is unhealthy," he told himself, referring, of course, to his thoughts. "They all look more like murderers than I. But that little gray man. . . . Ugh! How looks do deceive one . . ."

"Eh? Oh! Yes, it does seem warm," and the cashier gave him his change.

Charles had stared. "I must stop talking aloud like that," he warned himself as he swung out into the Avenue.

"And I must stop thinking in that way. . . . But I did pull the switch. I did pull the switch!"

◆

Windows, glittering magnetically, flaked the air like tangents of other spheres piled tier on tier above him marched converging before him. It was a crooning of motor axles coiling springlike outward along the stiff radial spoke to the oily suck and slurrr, the rubber-and-asphaltum churn that grinds no corn and mills no grain but only the smooth cars flashing brass-and-glass-and-varnish-bright. Keen-snouted phalanxes routing the wind, their prey, down the Avenue; and Charles Dograr.

"Fed herself (himself likewise?" said he) "into the vast conveyorbelt of plate-glass windows blue signs. . . ." (as if out of a bubble remembering) the air piping clear; the street a spoke of the sun: but (he could not remember (except an empty gray-dusted room) and why? when? where? became the tall doorman in blue (blue signs? blue signs?) handing the fat lady to her motor) an armored truck went by.

He recalled he had not slept: the inharmonious night pulling him almost physically backward with a drooping revulsion into (what? when? who?) some unremembered dream? some unvisited locality? Had not some forgotten woman breathed the silver mail of her soul about him?

He was walking up Fifth Avenue: the pistoning men, aptly moving, glozed with women as with oil.

They were all taking themselves so seriously.

The moment past, Charles Dograr made himself serious. He swung his arms like the rest. He masked a face of "It's 4:37 now and I've got to be at the offices of the Hydraulic Compression and Resurfacing Company 999 West 48 Street at 11:30" over his whimpering soul. Resolutely he projected himself past the Astor Library.

He crawled down the blustering length of Third Avenue, passing, one by one, like an inch-worm on a yardstick, the calipering legs of the El. He turned a corner. Suddenly he remembered his sixty dollars.

He went into a drugstore and had a malted milk and a cream cheese sandwich. Then he went to Weber and Heilbroner's and bought six silk shirts ($4.40 each with two collars to match in the Manhattan Manner) light blue with white pin stripes really a charming effect very exclusive. Passing a five-and-ten-cent store he went in and bought several key rings, an egg beater, three can openers and a string of imitation pearls.

He had some vague idea of laying these, a votive offering, on the steps of the lady across the way. It must be remembered that he had not yet met Adeline. However, half an hour later, he had tossed all the bundles into a deserted garbage wagon on East Sixty-Third Street.

◈

It was a dead time. Forty-Second Street bored him.

He went up to Columbus Circle and stared with yellow eyes into the Park. He imagined himself a patient in Bellevue Hospital.

"What I really ought to do," he said to himself, "is go to college."

A strange sense of peace swooped with white wings upon him—a solemnity causeless and absurd but lovely like white clouds in the sky—a peace that drifted, inwardly voluted, that lolled apart and drifted like clouds merging and separating again—and he stood silently on the street corner, wondering at the functions of the human body. He marvelled that the man who lies down in a field of growing grain can ever arise again.

"Decomposition so intricately prolonged. A process of rot ingeniously subdivided and balanced against itself so that one part feeds on the decay of the other and man walks full seventy year. The vegetables are not vindictive," he said.

"Alive or dead," he told himself, "I am just so much manure. One hundred and sixty-five pounds of it, belonging by right to the nearest field of corn. Take me out among the hills and lay me down there, a willing hostage from mankind, a tribute to the silent sway, the august overlordship of the Vegetable Kingdom.

"O mighty Milkweed, spare me now! Give ear, all-succoring and all-powerful Potato, to my plea and stay Thy hand that I may speak.

"For we, Thy servants, too long have spurned Thee; Thy slaves, we have abjured Thee, flouting Thy high commands.

"And the spirit of Evil has grown strong within us, so that we scorned Those that were merciful to us and despised Them in whose mighty hands we are as dust.

"We have grown fat in the plenty Ye have afforded unto us; in the time of plenty we have forgotten the bitterness of Thy wrath, too long withheld. And a darkness has fallen upon our souls; and the puny power within us vaunteth itself.

"With the empty air are our bodies puffed up. Yea, even with empty air have we swelled up our souls, so that we cried for all Earth to hear that we are Earth's masters.

"And we have turned to the Heavens, the Unknown and Unknowable. 'Look up!' we cried in our boasting. 'Look up to Heaven. There find ye light!' forgetting that inward Light Ye gave us, warming our bellies, and threading our veins with life.

"We have turned from the Known to the Unknowable: we have taken the Unassimilable for the Assimilable. And our bodies are broken; and our spirits cast down. And of right shall Thy bitterness fall upon us; of right shall Thy wrath be loosed.

"But here cometh one who shall be Thy bondsman always. In all ways shall his spirit follow Thee; and his body gladly will he sacrifice unto Thee, that his body may be Thy body, and his soul Thy soul.

"Let his heart lie among the roots of the Elm-

Tree, that his soul may rise among Its branches.

"Let his loins lie among the roots of the Green Corn, and his reins among the roots of the Gooseberry Bush, that his soul may flower and give fruit with Them.

"Let the flesh of his legs lie among the roots of the Tomato Vine, that his soul may prosper with Them.

"Let the flesh of his arms lie among the roots of the Wheat-Stalk; and his brain lie among the roots of the Mountain Laurel; and the flesh of his thighs among the roots of the Fir-Tree; and the bones of his body among the roots of the Green Grass, that his soul may live and flourish with Them, through all Eternity.

"Here cometh one among you, proclaiming you King, that his soul may be assoiled.

Amen.   Amen.   Amen"

And he added: "*En ceste foy je vueil vivre et mourir.*"

At that moment a man with a washable necktie and a brown suit bumped against him. There was a swimming moment and buildings rocking. Charles slammed into him with both fists. Fifteen or twenty passers-by paused. Charles turned to them.

"This man would drag down the Fair Name of American Womanhood into the Mire of Infamy," he proclaimed, pointing to his recumbent antagonist. "Bearing the outward semblance of Honor, Uprightness, and the Spirit of Fair-Play that is typical of American Manhood, he worms his way into the sanctity of the American Home, and there works his foul way unobserved. That man—," he drew himself to his full height— "was trying to get my wife to run away with him. And besides, he's a Communist!"

A confused murmur rose from the hoarse throats of the crowd—a mingling of cheers for Charles, and threats for the unconscious victim. Charles with charming modesty, raised a deprecative hand and vanished in the direction of the Grand Central.

The afternoon editions were out. Hot from the presses, they had the results of the first two races at the Belmont Track, the Giants-Red Sox score through the fourth inning, and a telephotograph, rather blurred, of a wreck on the Santa Fe, near Baker, Idaho.

This much on the front page. Charles took a copy of the *Journal* and walked to a seat in the men's waiting room. He felt he must sit down. He had an odd feeling, as if he had drunk too much water. The room was humming like Judgement Day and spurting with light and

JERSEY MAN SLAIN BY UNSEEN HAND

Falls By Murder Bolt As Friend Looks On

New Killing Baffles Police Seek Morning Mystery-Visitor

Early this morning, as he sat in the library of his home at 133 Hillcrest Terrace, Union Hill, with James Larton, his lifelong friend and fellow-astronomer, Death struck to the brain of Edward B. Trulge, retired business man, member of one of New Jersey's oldest families and amateur student of astronomy, leaving him lifeless.

It was not the bullet, not the knife that cut him down. It was a weapon invisible as the wind, swift as the lightning, incredible as a fairy tale come true. Edward Trulge is the first victim of a method of murder which, if the prognostics of Captain M. R. Stope, Chief of the Union Hill

"Well, I suppose it's not so important beside the affairs of a nation but they gave a lot of space to "It is possible? A whole column!" A tinkle of exultation falling in an icebox he felt sweat

Police, called hurriedly to the scene, are true, marks the beginning of a carnival of crime unparalleled in the history of the world.

Edward Trulge was electrocuted by an electric discharge coming no one knows how from no one knows where. The whole interior of his skull was literally cooked like the contents of a crucible, set in an electric furnace. According to the opi
far as can at
lacking more
5000 degrees cen
As h
finrst face clapped

    a blue black mark on his
      only   certain a man
  has le   he secret of
the lightning d   dcontrit at
  no ot   ay   hanwe expn
  When the surg   scalped revealed the interi   of theddnd
burned to a cris   Comwhe
estim at   onfas   enou
core of a   stricke
ssioner Ho GOD! with no
known forc   ve one
ere someh elive fiend in
can contr power for evil
  hellish   hearconveiceert
    eert cannoavenafter
      I willing
      o enemies
        timevebeena

     Fire

    cold-white his face tangibly like glue to his gums and his nose it was cutting his brain "It is cutting my brain! My

    face like oil white they must see!" he was clinging to the paper as to the gunwale of a ship. His intestines a cold "So this is it! So this is it!" He set himself doggedly to endure.

    God!

    was glutting his intestines; wrapped coldly his throat in a pulsing hand and "I must get out" stupidly conceived the floor to be walkable. Somewhere back of his thought the room made a switching turn and there were suddenly great bulging noises his heels drumming his ears and faces ballooning upward horrifiedly he made a sickening attempt to wave his hand and for a moment the ceiling collapsed upward, fringing.

He was lying flat on his back. His hand hurt and his head hurt. He seemed to remember having seen a naked old man in a bathtub and a man bent above him.

"Are you Cousin Herbert? I'm Foster."

The man was evidently very excited and quite pale and it seemed to Charles unnecessarily fussy.

"I don't know how I'd have found you if I hadn't been right here when you fell and seen you reading the paper. Isn't it terrible? We should have told you more in the telegram. Such a shock! Such a shock! Here, can't you help me lift him up to a seat instead of standing around there? Easy, now. He's just had a terrible shock."

"Now," he suddenly sat down and Charles felt little brown eyes like lead pencils leaving marks all over him. "Can you walk? Can you get to a taxi?"

Charles felt his brain within his unobedient body gnawing like a ferret at the man's words.

"So you're Cousin Foster?" he ventured.

"Yes. And we thought I'd meet you at the train to break it to you. But I must have missed you. And then I walked through the station and just by good fortune I was passing. God! Such a shock! And can you imagine us this morning when they told us what had happened to him? For a moment when I saw you fall with the paper in your hand I thought you were another one. Here! Taxi!"

And inexplicably, standing in front of Liggett's Drugstore, on that busy corner, he began to weep, his cheeks wrinkling up into little furrows.

"I came on the 9:35," Charles ventured, analytically.

"Oh! Yes, yes! Terrible! Terrible!" he blubbered while the taxi driver stared in amazement.

"The first train I could get," Charles hardly knew what to do. He couldn't cry with him. He put his arm around his shoulder. "Every one is terribly upset. Cheer up. Cheer up."

The driver was leaning around in his seat to catch the address. "Where to?"

Charles waited. Now he'd find out. "Where to?"

Foster glanced at Charles and then blurted, "Union Hill. 133 Hillcrest Terrace."

Seated side by side with the son of his victim, Charles Dograr was riding to the home of the murdered man!

IV—FROM A SCOTLAND YARD DOCKET

THE most diligent search in all directions by a trained body of experts has been comparatively barren of information as to the past of the singular old gentleman with whom, at the lodging house of West Twenty-Third Street, New York, Charles Dograr began his curious adventure.

"At the time of which we write, he was known in the lodging house above referred to as Mr. Constantin. To the curious he gave out that he was a retired professor of chemistry from a Western university. He admitted to a hobby for photography. There is ground for belief that he was born in Bâle, Switzerland, of an upper-class bourgeois family. His father was a dealer in curios and old books. He was educated in Lausanne. Upon leaving there, he spent six years at Oxford, specializing in the Eastern languages.

His career at the English university was un-marked by any irregularity.

"That, at some stage of his career, he had kept many a lonely vigil beside the heavy-shouldered, the ruffian sea, the ruffed and petticoated, cream-ing sea, its void immensity (perhaps in the qual-ity of a Life Guard on the New England coast whose rocks rise stark from the billows) no one who has ever looked into his hawk-hooded eyes can doubt. At what time this was, however, one can only conjecture. After his death (the spec-tacular details of which, as will be recorded later in these pages, were given perhaps undue prom-inence in the newspapers not only of New York but of all the other large American cities as well) a certain Mrs. Aht of Erie, Pa., laid claim to his estate, alleging that, after living with her as man and wife during seven years, he had deserted her and their two children in June, 1908. She de-scribed his profession as that of a stone mason.

"He was recognized, though disguised as a bishop, at the Polo Grounds, New York, by Operative B639, who had had occasion to know him in India during the Hillfield uprisings, of which he was supposed to have been the moving cause. Simultaneously with his residence on West Twenty-Third Street (and his participation in the singular events the recital of which make up the body of this chronicle) a certain Thorndyke Smithers was holding open house in one of Long Island's most palatial residences.

"His apparent profession was that of a stock broker. He was daring behind the hounds; despite his advanced age, he was noted for his recklessness on the polo field. He drank deep and hearty. By these traits, as well as by the unprecedented magnificence of an unending series of fêtes and festivals given on the lawns or in the halls of his mansion, this Thorndyke Smithers had attained to undoubted leadership in the faster set of suburban society. He was none other than the old gentleman with whom we have affair.

"A curious type in the annals of criminology! In a letter to a friend in Kratensberg, dated from Bellow's Falls, Vermont, and found among his effects after his death, the following unusual phrase appears: 'God knows, if ever a gutta-percha soul resided in an India-rubber body, that man is I.' This is especially curious in that the reverse would seem to be true. He was always intriguing. An acquaintance states that he once saw the old gentleman, opening a borrowed book, find a visiting card, left as a place-marker, between the leaves. The name printed thereon was: M. Carlos Becerra. Upon observing it, the old gentleman fell into a revery lasting a full half hour, from which he roused himself to favor the acquaintance there present with a long and exceedingly learned disquisition on the waning ideals of human greatness. Upon the friend's observing, 'Egad, Tom, I'd no idea you were a classical scholar!' the old gentleman responded pithily and, as it turned out, significantly, 'The classics, if not the butter, are certainly the bread of my daily life.'

"Meantime, the residents of exclusive Thirty-Eighth Street had occasion to smile at the harmless eccentricities of the aged inhabitant of a dark old house near the corner of Madison Avenue. He wore shell-rimmed spectacles, wheeled himself about in a bathtub-shaped, rub-

ber-tired contrivance and received no one,
though truckloads of canned pears arrived daily
at the back entrance. He passed his days sitting
at an upper-story window, tearing up bits of
paper and throwing them into the street with
inconceivable rapidity, and in such quantities
that on some afternoons the tiny particles lay to
a depth of three inches on the sidewalk before
the house and traffic through the street was seriously impeded. Again, it was the old gentleman.
In this identity, he posed as M. Carolo Faudras,
Ex-Ambassador to Sweden, though what nation
he had represented was never revealed.

"He had a habit of wiping his left eyebrow
with his right forefinger. This gesture became
almost frenzied at the crisis of the cytherean
moment. It was by this fact that he was recognized by Fraülein Netta Felder, the singer, in
Sofia, during the Fall of 1906. He had also a
liking amounting almost to an obsession for
Washington pie.

"After the downfall of the Crime Ring in
New York, of which he was the acknowledged
head, trunk lines capable of carrying a current of

700,000 amperes were discovered, leading to all of his various residences from the power-houses of the Addington Power and Light Company, Flushing, Long Island. For what purpose these were designed is not known but the directors of the Addington Co. were indicted and held as accessories before the fact in his crimes. The trial is still pending.

"Two photographs of him, as far as is known, are alone extant. One, taken at about the age of twenty-five, shows him, in white serge and a yachting cap, promenading before the Café de Paris, at Cannes. The other, taken perhaps fifteen years later, shows him as one of an ensemble taken of the participants in a fancy dress ball, where and exactly when not known. He wears the costume of a Hindu Rajah, with turban, fisbah, pantaloons and ceremonial sword thrust in a jewelled sash. He stands behind and a little apart from the rest, with his arm thrown over the shoulder of a naked model.

"He was tried: in Paris, August 1895, for arson and manslaughter; Vienna, March 1899, attempted rape; Chicago, October 1904, shoplifting and barratry; Edgewater, Illinois, in 1904, drunkenness, obscene language and resisting arrest; El Paso, Texas, January 1907, conducting a game of chance; St. Petersburg, July 1911, attempting to cash non-valid checks; at Brussels, August 1911, complicity in the attempt to rob the Burgenhaus Bank; Lyon, France, September 1919, forging identification papers; Calcutta, July 1921, running a house of prostitution without a license. In each case he received a verdict of acquittal. . . ."

So much and no more shall we quote from the Scotland Yard Docket. Little as it is, and small an insight as it affords into the man's character, it is all that the greatest detective organization in the world could discover about the strange man —Benjamin Constantin, Thorndyke Smithers, Prince Eugène de Montenegro, Carolo Faudras, E. Burke, Wynn Holcomb, René Fonstant, Edouard Percy, Aaron Glemby, Comte de la Birette, Thomas Malling or Thomas Wallace—call him what you will—who now sits in the room on Twenty-Third Street, methodically planning the greatest coup of his career!

V—"YOU ARE NOT COUSIN HERBERT!"

Bᴜᴛ first (and in New York Charles Dograr riding) the Seine behind the gleaming bridges was a long blue laugh through the painted lattices of a window (blue blue-green green-yellow but a scum of scarlet filtering the trees) purple-blue blue-green (beneath the red strake of a (for a (yes) moment the blue the) barge plugs the yawning bridge and a woman in a black petticoat: she stacks a dumpy figure against the thrust of a tiller: and then (oddly) life is empty again all empty and:

Thought, action, the drifting inconsequent activities of men women horticulturally re-peopling the streets men women drifting (even the vociferous buildings (gray-blue) the siren-ing spire of Sainte Chapelle drifting) a moment and:

Lolling fading into the vacuous wide inviting

smile green blue-green gray-blue of the (yes)
Seine was a scimitar; the dark air curved beneath
its destructive blade but:

Hastily she remembered the chocolates not
that life matters but:

She turned away but:

It cannot be said that Charles Dograr had the
faintest perception or apperception of all this.
Not the distance that separated them (Paris from
New York is approximately 4,377 miles, plotted
on the slum-sline); not a disparity in time (for
the two events, computed to meridian time, will
be found to have taken place at the same moment); nor the difference, real or apparent, in
location and situation between the two can be
urged in explanation or mitigation of the fact.
For, unquestionably, the lady who walked the
bridges of the Seine and looked down into its
lucent waters and thought of the drifting lives
of men and women and started back at last from
the horror of suicide—that woman was thinking
of Charles Dograr.

But for Charles Dograr, riding in the taxi
with Foster the son of Edward Trulge, it was

only as if one segment of his brain were rapt in a dream his grosser senses could but hint at—in a flash of wheels axles turning thin horns piping (against the Macy's sign)—in an unrememberable glimpse of blue fading and deepening to purple and netted dripping in scarlet (into the screech along the rotted shoring as the ferry nosed bluntly into its slip):

Reader, have you ever felt (the stiffthroated buildings, the ironcoursing streets fading before your eyes) that you were but the semblance of another's dream? Has it seemed (your vision bursting for a moment into keen nothingness) that you were but the lymph in the organs of some gigantic creature's being, your whole life but a gesture of that organism's functioning? Has it come to you, sometimes, to have been swept by the breath of a woman's passing—some unknown woman, perhaps, who had come to you in dreams but with face always averted and now (for a moment) you are caught in the golden tissue of her hair, you are filled with a rich and elusive perfume—for a moment only, and she passes unseen unheard, and you are whirling again in the spate of the crowd?

So Charles Dograr. He thought it was God. He was wrong.

But he left it all, unheeding, in one small bubbling corner of his brain. Moments were precious now.

Discreetly questioning Cousin Foster, he had learned:

1. Cousin Herbert (ex tem. Charles Dograr) lived in Bridgeport, Conn. He had two aunts, Mary and Louise.

2. Uncle Edward, (the murdered man) always wore blue socks.

3. Cousin Herbert studied architecture. He had a dog named Shep.

4. His name was Herbert Trask. He had been a favorite with Uncle Edward because both had a weakness for astronomy.

5. He (Herbert) had not visited Union Hill for seven years. He would be surprised how it had grown up.

6. Adeline had been in Bridgeport last summer to visit Herbert's mother.

7. Old Mr. Carroll drank as much as ever.

8. Adeline was Adeline Laggick. She was also a niece of Trulge, but on the mother's side.

9. Mr. Larton had left the Repeater Coin-Filling Company and was now with the Spencer Eye-Dropper Corp.

Things fringed. Herbert had apparently once lived (10) on a farm, because Foster talked of the summer he had spent visiting them, when they had jumped into the pigpen and tried to play toreador with the sow.

"Of course. Of course," assented Charles. "Lord, how long ago that seems, though. How many years was it, anyway?" seeking verification.

But Foster was of that curious type who have so solemn a concept of Time that they lapse into an awed silence whenever a date or term of years is mentioned. Now he went into a kind of cogitative trance, pointing his eyes down his nose.

"Why, let's see—it was four years ago when we went up to Worcester and I remember Aunt May saying at the time that . . ." (Stick to

Uncle Edward's blue socks and (Out of the debris of information he had received Charles was beginning to construct a kind of trestlebridge across the abyss of danger that confronted him and) "How is Aunt Mary? Doing well?" . . . and he would be back at night to the old gentleman with a grand tale to tell. But—sucking like a sponge at his stomach as his mind span to a thin bright disk—was this girl Adeline! A dark-faced sallow-haired girl (so he saw her) sitting in a Morris chair and apparently she had seen the real Herbert last summer in Bridgeport. She leaps to her feet as he enters the door, points an accusing finger. . . . (In the meantime they were climbing a long hill above railroad yards. A river. . . .) What to do with Adeline? . . .) ". . . and yet it couldn't have been 1910 because I . . . West Virginia so I suppose . . . I swear, Herbert, you've got me all mixed up. It seems it must have been 1909, but if . . ."

"1907!" Charles dumped out of his mouth like a piece of indigestible pudding. Foster took it up and chewed it. "Let's see. I'd have been seven years old. That don't seem . . ."

And then the brass doorknob! The Colonial porch! Inside, there would be red curtains. . . .

The brass doorknob swung in. There were red curtains. A long hall. Charles was sure he had uttered a slight cry. He found himself shaking hands with a B-shaped lady dressed in black. "Aunt Louise, this is Herbert. I found him in the Grand Central. He fainted. Say, Aunt Louise, when did we go up to Hawk Center to see Herbert? 1909?"

"How is Aunt Mary? Doing well?" asked Charles mechanically, in a faint voice.

The wallpaper was the most vivid thing in the room where they had ushered him. At regular intervals across an expanse of cottony carpet the furniture erected itself, like tombstones in a churchyard, with an air of gloomy but indomitable insistence. All the rest of the family were drawn up to receive him in a bay window around a fern standing in a hammered brass tabouret. It gave the impression that every other room in the ponderous and moldering house was empty.

All sensation of pity or of repugnance vanished from Charles' heart.

"This is Mr. Constable. I don't think you ever met him but you must have heard Edward—poor . . . ("Dear Edward I can't imagine . . . ("Oh! If the police would only . . . ("Now now you know that Mr. Larton . . . (An as yet unidentified lady in a checked taffeta blouse burst into violent tears and Charles rivetting) . . . said that they are nothing more than a pack of . . .") . . . do something about . . .") . . . how any one could have . . .") . . . dear Edward he spoke of him often." Charles did not hear.

His attention had been caught by a series of rhythmic and resounding thumps that appeared to emanate, through the ceiling of the room, from the floor above. A vague premonition prompted him to speak.

"Where is Cousin Adeline?" he asked. At this moment, the thumping stopped. Every one appeared disconcerted.

"We must get him some tea," remarked Aunt Janet, as if she had been nudged from behind.

"I *said* somebody ought to get poor Herbert

some food. I *told* you when I came in how he fainted in the railway station."

"Where is Cousin Adeline?" he had asked.

"Louise, won't you go out and see if there isn't some of that nice veal pie left?"

Obscuring more and more of vine-and-bird-and-flower wallpaper in geometric ratio as his form advanced, Mr. Constable set himself in motion toward our hero. There was something reminiscent of the blanket held before a bull in his manner and Charles sensed suddenly that by his question he had in some way frightened them, and that to Mr. Constable's board-of-director's-meeting manner had been left the explication by the rest.

"You have often, doubtless, heard, Cousin— may I, too, share the honor of relationship— though only temporarily—in the Trulge family at this moment of affliction?—Cousin Herbert, in I am sure your wide acquaintance with the literature, not only of this day, but of other generations and other ages, the story of the clown, the clown who bleeds as he laughs, smiles as he weeps? Pagliacci—that grandest, to my mind, of Puccini's operatic compositions—is the most famous example of the timeworn situation —so timeworn, in fact, that we are apt, in hastily condemning it as trite, to lose all sight of the fundamental truth . . ."

Charles, with his nose for paradox, could not help here sniffing a new trail.

"A truth, too often repeated, becomes by the fact, untrue: you wish to say?" he queried.—"I must interrupt to thank you for leading my mind to the consideration of the curious phenomenon. Though until this moment it had escaped my attention it is, on the face of things at least, an indisputable verity.

"In Art, of course . . ." he went on, meditatively. "Truth, decreasing in its enunciation; it is an awesome thought. And in life . . . Truth, a mental suit of clothes, to be outgrown —or, as you put it, outworn. Truth—the distillate of needs, desires, customs themselves transitory, building on the Truths they have brought forth. Truth—the milk of the cow, if the cow itself fed on that milk. Truth—the coral island,

if the polyps themselves inhabited it." He seized
Mr. Constable's amazed hand.

"It is, sir, a holy thought. The Well of Truth!
. . . Of course. How wise, sir, were the ancients!
A well runs dry with too much drinking.

"And one can continue," he continued.
"Truth, like all things else, fatigues itself in repe-
tition. The secret of revolution. One verges, perhaps unwisely but as always with new systems,
on an attempt to define the motivation of all
human progress. The truth of mortal ethics—a
carpenter's rule, measuring the path to Eternity.
The carpenter, Man, marks the edge with
his finger, and advances the ruler another
length. . . ."

"Exactly. Exactly," Mr. Constable cut in, and
Charles saw the man had entirely missed the
point. "One cannot too often confirm a thing
that is true. And here, as it happens,—in this
house, we have an example. For at this moment
—if at this hallowed time I may use a profane
illustration—we find ourselves, so to speak, back-
stage, at the moment when Pagliacci, in this case

a feminine one, must distill laughter from her tears.

"The loved one is dead; the family cluster about the death-bed. . . . Pagliacci's heart is breaking. . . . But the call sounds. The curtain is rising. The audience must be amused. The audience . . . must be . . ." It appeared for a moment that Mr. Constable would be carried away in the sweep of his own emotions.

But he regained his voice and continued. "So Adeline—brave girl. No one, we all know, loved her Uncle more deeply, more truly than she. No one, we know as well, will more eternally perpetuate his memory in the shrine of a devoted heart. And yet—"

Aunt Janet suddenly thrust her face between them. "But folks might talk, y'know, if they knew. She's got to go on, though I always did say that a profession that the Church frowns on—"

The heavy tones of Mr. Constable steam-rollered her out of existence. "Exactly. Exactly. We who know her will venerate her fortitude the more highly. But the outsider, who might not know . . ."

Charles was utterly at sea.

At this moment, through the double door of the hallway, entered a girl—*the* girl, the beauty his soul, unknowing, had dreamed of. She was tall, long-limbed, smooth-moving. Her eyes were black, and sparkling. Caught negligently over the curve of one shoulder a silken scarlet cloak floated out in the speed of her graceful advance.

The other shoulder was bare. Bare, too, the firmly-modelled, branching slope from the creamy-columned throat downward to where a bandage of gilt cloth, woven with silver spangles, just confined the tender-pointed breasts. Thence downward, the pink-tinted, delectable torso was cobwebbed o'er with a veil of gossamer gauze (and the recreant orb of Charles caught unashamed in the network of imitation pearls sewn shimmering thereon) which fell, diaphanous and disarrayed, until a similarly-spangled gilt loincloth confined its wayward folds more closely about her marbled lower limbs.

"Adeline!" gasped an aunt.

"Tea?" cried she, uncomprehending.

Mr. Constable retained his grasp of the situation. "I have just," he began tactfully, "been telling Cousin Herbert of the inspiring similitude between the tale of Pagliacci and your devotion, in the face of your dear Uncle's demise, to your Oriental dances."

Her eye turned in Charles' direction, and a flush, deliciously delicate, mantled her glowing cheek. For a moment their eyes met, and a buzz of ardor leaped in his.

"Why—but—but—he is—why—" and then, searing, direct—"*You are not Cousin Herbert!*"

He leaped the window, sped across the lawn. Down the street to the corner—a passing trolley —a burst of speed. . . . Charles scrambled aboard, but even as his nickle tinkled in the fare-box, so a thought dropped ringing in his heart. Her tone—the words still sounded in his ears, the intonation would linger with him always—had there not, yes, had there not been a tinge of joy, like roselight across the eastern sky at dawning —a cadence in her voice as of Love surprised and palpitating?

VI—BARED FANGS

"B<small>UT</small> my dear," questioned Mrs. Taitch, "Are you not afraid?"

The two ladies are sitting over late tea, on the enclosed side-porch of the Pragman home in Yonkers. There are purple hills in the background, and the sun glows like magenta moonlight, with shadows reclining, chill, violet and still, behind the Dutch-cut trees that cluster in black-outlined groups among the deep-napped verdure. Far down the undulating valley-side, smoke rises from the chimney of a solitary farmhouse, stencilling fleetingly across the sunset clouds: "Buy Best's Coal—It's Best!"

"Don't be silly!" laughed Mrs. Pragman. But her voice trails golden into the silence that tottered, dense and precarious, over their heads. She had been talking at random, to gain time. Now, she raises her eyes and a silver wire of premonition tautens along the fused glances of the two women.

"I wonder," Mrs. Pragman wondered, "I wonder . . . my husband . . . can anything be . . . ?"

It was, as it happened, exactly 3:35 P. M.

❖

At 3:36, Mr. Randolph Flock, living at 842 East 75 St., coined the phrase: "You may have a barrel of money, but you look like a hogshead to me," which later won the $10,000 Slanguage Prize offered by the Daily News.

❖

At 3:37 a taxi turned the corner of Rivington Street into Allen. Midway in the block, a man stepped out of a real estate office. In the taxi, a man sitting beside the chauffeur turned to three men sitting in the tonneau.

"That's him! That's him!" he called excitedly. "Let him have it."

One gun jammed. The other two fired almost

simultaneously. Hit, the man on the sidewalk hurled himself toward the hallway.

"Give him the works, the bastard! Let him have it. Get him!"

A woman sitting in the apartment house door-way rose, leaned against the carved ornamental stone pilaster and collapsed. A stain widened hastily on the back of her cheap blouse. From within the hallway, the shot man was firing automatically. The cab took up speed, dodged a truck around the corner and toward the river.

❖

In the third car of a downtown express, wait-ing above the 96th Street station for a Bronx Express to clear, Lucius M. Pilbore looked at his watch. 3:38.

❖

At 3:39 the famous producer of the Vanmore Follies—Karyl Vanmore—finished telling the latest one to a group of friends sitting in the dark pit of a theater. He turned toward the stage, gummy with girls in tights, rompers, knickers and bathing suits.

"Let's see the big ones," he called.

A man in shirt sleeves and a checked cap, standing on the stage, was herding a file of mediums to the wings.

"Now stand here and keep together," he admonished them pettishly. "And you ones that Mr. Vanmore wanted to speak to later keep to this side. . . . Now the show-girls. All the show girls out here, please. . . . Hurry up now, d'you want us to send y'aninvitation?" A subdued titter ran among the girls.

Gradually a line of statuesque creatures formed along the footlights.

"Nobody that don't want to leave New York," counselled Mr. Vanmore. "Nobody that don't want to leave New York, Chapin."

"Nobody that don't want to leave New York," repeated Chapin. Two or three dropped out haughtily at this announcement.

Mr. Vanmore, standing with hands behind his back at the foot of the aisle, glanced along the row of faces. "Why, hello, Amy. . . . Back again, Melissa. . . . Here's Teddy, too. . . . All the old familiar faces. . . . How are you, Snoots?"

"Just fine, Mr. Vanmore," the girl's voice sounded ludicrously feeble in the empty theater. All the others were nodding and simpering.

"All right." He was suddenly and—as is the privilege of a famous producer—untransitionally brusk. "Let's have some music." A tinny piano in the wings struck up a waltz. "Well, now, girls. Walk. Keep time. . . ." They started in a slow prancing circle. . . . "A little slower Chapin."

"A little slower, Jerry," Chapin relayed it to the piano man.

◇

At 3.40 the dumbwaiter bell rang in an apartment on West 119 Street. Mrs. Flakkan answered the call by opening the dumbwaiter door.

"Meat ma-a-an," came the call up the stale-flavored shaft.

"Send it up," she called back. "It should 'a been here a half hour ago."

◇

At 3:41, Charles Dograr opened the door of Room 407 L. H. Sykes & Co, Hotel Agency, in a building on West Twenty-Ninth Street and walked up to the girl at the switchboard.

"May I speak to Mr. Rupert Pragman?" he asked politely. "It's very important."

"Pragman? Pragman? . . . Yasure itain Board-man?" the girl asked. "There don nobody uh thaname woik here."

"No, it's Pragman."

"Well, there donobody name Pragman woik here."

He went out to the corridor. It was the seventh office he had tried. But the man must work somewhere in the building.

Room 409

ART-TEX Kraft Rugs

J. R. Kennedy, N. Y. Mgr.

He opened the door. A fat man sitting behind coils of cigar smoke glanced up at him inquiringly. The window was grimy.

"Is there a Mr. Rupert Pragman working in this office?"

The man moved his head slowly from side to

side, then turned his gaze toward a large illustrated calendar on the wall.

"Thank you," said Charles Dograr, and went out.

Room 411

Buckeye Belt and Leather Corpn.

F. S. Knox, Prest.

A girl peered out from beneath a sign Information.

"May I see Mr. Pragman—Rupert Pragman?"

"Pragman . . . he's in Shipping, isnee?"

"I—I think so," agreed Charles affably.

The girl had her lips to the phone and was twiddling a little switch back and forth.

"H'lo—Hello—H'lo. . . . Ship*ping?* . . . Wll, is thera Rupert Pragman out there? . . . Yes, wll . . . there's a genlmnoutere wansa see'm. . . . What name please? . . . *What name please?*" Charles, who had been sinking into almost dozy restfulness after his search, perceived that the girl had deflected her thin-edged voice toward him.

"Name? . . . Ah . . . Foster . . . ah . . .

Foster," he produced, and added, "From the Merchant's Mercantile Association."

The girl had turned to the phone again. "Itsa Mister Fawster R. Fawster . . . yais . . . a awri-i . . ." She was looking at Charles again. "He'll be ou'," she promised. "They donusually let tha cleyks comouthough, doorinawfisours. . . ."

"Oh?"

There were a few sweetish-tasting moments of waiting, then:

"Mr. Pragman, good-afternoon."

"I—I think you must have the wrong man. I —I—" Pragman produced the words, like a magician so many rabbits, from his throat.

"Oh! No. After our little conversation of this morning, I confess, there might seem little reason for consulting you further. But our policy, sir, is Thoroughness, and we felt we could not act without seeing you again."

"I—I—I—" he was cut off again.

"Quite! Quite!" said Charles Dograr, suddenly assuming an English accent. "If you will step outside to the corridor, where we can talk with perhaps greater freedom, I shall be glad to go further into the matter with you . . . (They were at the door. 'If I go out he'll kill me! If I don't I'll my job he'll kick up a row and I'll lose my. . . . .') . . . certain aspects of the question that are still in need of elucidation."

Glassily moving, Rupert Pragman found they were out in the corridor. Once the door of:

Room 411
Buckeye Belt and Leather Corpn.
F. S. Knox, Prest.

had closed behind them, the disgusting man suddenly seized Pragman's arm and burst into laughter. It was full five minutes before he could control himself, and then his words came brokenly between little hiccoughs of merriment, his voice was weak, his face suffused as of a man who has spent himself with laughing during an evening of delightful, clean entertainment at

PALACE THEATER
High-Class Vaudeville

He ceased as suddenly as he had begun.

"Where do you live?" he asked.

The abruptness of the question caught Pragman off guard. Before he could prevent himself, "97 Juniper Street, Yonkers, New York," he had answered.

"Good!" Charles Dograr had become brisk and businesslike. "You are wondering, no doubt, why I venture to intrude myself and my affairs upon you during the busiest hours of your no doubt very fully occupied day. I shall intrude only in the extent to which these affairs concern you."

He poked an admonitory finger against Pragman's breast pocket and his eye hypnotically he continued. "Of the extent in which they do concern you, my dear sir, you are probably not as yet aware. It is my business to inform you.

"As for the 'Merchants' Mercantile Association,' your detective instinct—which, à propos (the French words giving a velvety touch to the dialogue) I am delighted, judging from the admirable manner in which you carried off the surprise of our rencontre before the telephone girl in the office, to find developed to an unusually (if I may say so) high degree—will tell you that it was but a ruse to justify my presence.

"In fact, sir, my impression of you has been so favorable—vide: one:—(Charles checking off the factors on his fingers as he spoke) your courage and *insouciance* this morning; two:—your quick-wit and *savoir-faire* this afternoon—that it shall be my pleasant duty to report you to the Chief as one most eminently fitted for induction into our organization, and as one thoroughly equipped with the qualifications necessary to the man who will be entrusted with the problem of solving what is perhaps the greatest murder mystery of all time."

Pragman's face gaped before him like the slot of the ornamental letterboxes designed for the Sunset Drive in Sacramento, California. Charles, sensing his ascendancy, paused and drew himself to his full height before he continued.

"I refer, of course—and the secrecy necessary to be observed with regard to this highly confidential statement will mark the implicit trust we place, sir, in you—to the Trulge murder, a case to the solution of which our organization has been called because the police not only of New York but of all the other metropolisses—(Charles had not been sure of the plural form of this word, but he carried it off—he carried it off)— of the world are completely at sea. When can you begin?"

Words (apologies to Ronald Firbank) fluttered like pink butterflies joyously from Pragman's mouth.

"Are you—are you—" he asked, "from the Searchlight Detective Agency and Training School?"

Charles' heart leaped proud within him. It had not, after all, been a wrong guess. He had made it a toss-up between scenario-writing and detectives.

"Exactly! Exactly!" he replied on a note of enthusiasm. "I knew I could count on you to understand. At times, in the study of our thorough-going course in detecting in all its phases, your determination may have weakened, the light may have grown dim before your eyes. But now, now!—now!—you see the reward!"

And—"The Reward!"—he repeated, producing the badge which, like the good strategist he was, he had been careful to procure beforehand.

"You are now,"—pinning the medal to Pragman's vest—"an operative of the Searchlight Detective Agency, empowered, at home and abroad, to retain, suborn, interrogate, replevin, and proceed to the arrest to, from and of all malefactors, criminals *or* suspected malefactors or criminals *or* other persons known or for good reasons supposed to be enemies of the Body General, by these presents be it resolved.

"Your salary will be from $3000 to $5000 a year!

"All expenses will be paid!

"You will travel!

"You will see the world!"

He paused. Pragman's heart, like a Strasbourg goose's liver, was feeding on his words.

"Quit your job tonight. Give your employer any excuse you may think of.

"At an hour as yet undetermined, but for the present to be denominated as 'X,' I or another operative empowered to treat with you will visit you at your home at 97 Juniper Street, Yonkers, New York!

"Hold yourself in readiness!

"You will recognize the visitor by the password—'Eggs are indeterminate but fowls are firm.' The operative will reply—'If Moscow reverses, sell at once'!

"Accept no substitute!

"Have you studied the Trulge case?"

Pragman shook his head, chagrined. For a permissible moment, Charles Dograr looked stern. "You must keep *au courant*," he admonished at last, relenting.

He thrust a copy of the *Evening Journal* into Pragman's hands.

"Here! Study this! A detailed report and instructions will be handed you by the operative referred to!

"Meantime. . . Secrecy! . . . Watchfulness! . . . Eternal Vigilance!"

A fleeting handclasp, warm with friendliness, strong with resolution. . . .

A word: "We depend on you!"

And Rupert Pragman rubberly was trying to open the familiar

Room 411
Buckeye Belt and Leather Corpn.
F. S. Knox, Prest.

Charles Dograr had vanished toward the elevators.

VII—LIGHT THROUGH FOG

"Y OU will observe, then——," the old gentleman halted suddenly, looking down at his young disciple. "Have you plenty of paper?" he asked.

"Oh! Yes! Yes!" said Charles Dograr, all agog to continue the fascinating lesson.

"Hm-m-m-m-m. It may seem that we start rather far afield, but have I proved my fundamental thesis: that Metaphysics, per se, is intrinsically as precise a science as Physics, since, granting the division of the senses, each derives, by the same means, from the Science of Ontology? [1]

"Yes," said Charles Dograr.

"I think I stated too," continued the old gentleman, "the curious fact—simple enough, but so often overlooked—defining the difference be-

[1] Springart and Carm, *The Physicist's Handbook*, (Cincinnati, 1914) pp. 137-5; Gogorza, *La Esencia de las Ciencias*, (Valladolid, 1743) vol. 8, ch. xliii.

tween these two sciences, namely: that both, though proceding by directly parallel methods, make use of absolutely complementary human equipment—if I may so state it.

"Roughly, one depends on the mind to the exclusion, if possible, of the senses—the other on the senses to the exclusion, if possible, of the mind. And *entre parenthèses*, I may say that the bastard pseudo-science of Psychology falls between two stools when it tries to straddle the difference."

"Oh!" said Charles Dograr.

"Now, when two instruments operate by the same method on the same subject, the difference in result, obviously, will be the measure of the difference in accuracy between the two instruments. In our case, physics and philosophy are the two instruments. The difference between the definitions of identical objects or phenomena as stated by each of the two sciences, then becomes an exact indication of the discrepancies in coordination between the mind and senses of man as at present functioning.

"We can," he picked up a half-eaten pork

chop and began idly gnawing it as he continued,
"go further. Using this difference as a base, we
can, by a process of mental triangulation [2] similar to that by which the surveyor estimates im-
mensurable distances, conjecture the point at
which the two sciences will converge into unity.

"For, obviously, if the two are homogeneous
in nature and homogenous in growth, the pin-
point of perfection in both (and consequently
in man's functioning) will be the moment at
which each merges into the other.

"Moreover, it is my firm belief that the best
way to advance our comprehension of the inter-
relation between the two sciences is by formulat-
ing—just as the economists with their *homo
œconomicus*—a conjectural *homo physico-philosophicus*, thus predicating, at the very begin-

[2] Federman, *Die Farbrelationem von Raum*, (Leipzig, 1878) p. 57. . .
"*durch die sinnliche Relation des aus der dreidimensionalen Gliederung
gewonnen Koordinationssystems. . . .*" etc. There are interesting fore-
shadowings of this theory among many earlier students, vide: Lucian,
De Scientia Libidinis, (Ms. Bib. Nat. Par.) fol. V, pp. xxii-vi, cix-xx,
etc.; Hesser, *Zun Alkimie Fundalis*, (Antwerp 1532) who, thinking to
develop a system of alchemy, divined instead, almost miraculously, the
system of modern thought.

ning, the perfections that will accrue when the two sciences exact.[3]

"I am not the first, I may say," the old gentleman smiled deprecatingly, "to have advanced the possibilities of this method of procedure.[4] But to my knowledge," and his voice rose higher as he spoke, "I am the first who has ever pursued it to any practical end.

"We have established, then, the principal point to be understood in the consideration of my invention: That the *homo physico-philosophicus can exist,—that his mind and his senses will act and interact in complete harmony, and that therefor he can be defined as one to whom the Sciences of Physics and of Metaphysics will be synonymous!*"

In his excitement he threw aside the porkchop. "Can exist, did I say?" Leaning forward,

[3] The sense of this passage is obscure. Several variant readings have been proposed. G. C. K. suggests: . . . ."beginning, the exact perfections accrue to the two sciences." Camb. Ed. (L. L. J.) reads. . . ."beginning, the perfect science that this accretion will exact." We give the Ms. reading, though obviously perverted.—Editor.

[4] He refers undoubtedly to Florentia Guillamentius, from whose *Un Leocht Ser Zeltgeis*, (Amsterdam 1688), pp. 971-2, the passage is an almost exact transcription.

he emphasized each word of the sentence that follows by a light tap of the forefinger on the left breast of Charles Dograr. "He *does* exist! I am the *homo physico-philosophicus*—the first perhaps, that has ever existed in the history of man!" [5]

Charles silently raised a glass of sherry in homage, then drained it. The old gentleman continued.

"Let us now try to understand the hypothetical brain functioning of this man. I have already pointed out the curious fact that in their definition of matter, the Sciences of Physics [6] and Metaphysics [7] differ only in that the first states that some substance as yet undetermined, when combined with *energy*, produces objective phe-

[5] Excepting, possibly, Pythagoras. In this connection, a 64-page in-12 pamphlet, privately issued in New York, 1907, under the name of René Fonstant and entitled, "*The Kinetic Properties of Form*," may be mentioned. 'René Fonstant,' it will be remembered, was one of the aliases of the old gentleman. The book is an attempt to modernize the Pythagorean theory of metempsychosis, applying it as a key to the atomic theory.

[6] Benson and Hedges, *Tobacconist's Guide* (N. Y.).

[7] Thomas More, *De Dementia Mundis* (Oxford, 1577). *Book of Knowledge*, (Int. Book Corp., 1918), pp. 913-27, etc. The book is invaluable, its publishers assert.

nomena, while the second holds that the same substance, combined with *form*, produces the same result.

"Both, therefor, are negative definitions, and can most advantageously be stated thus:

(Physics):	Phenomena — Energy $=$ Matter	(A)
(Metaphys:)	Phenomena — Form $=$ Matter	(B)

"Observed phenomena and observed matter are obviously equivalent terms in equation (A) and in equation (B). We can, therefor, subtract equation (B) from (A), and reach the result:

$$\text{Form} - \text{Energy} = 0$$

"Or:

$$\text{Form} = \text{Energy''}\ [8]$$

"Really," said Charles Dograr. "I never was very mathematical." He was beginning to feel

[8] As a matter of fact, the invention of various mechanical devices in which the utilization of force engendered was pushed to hitherto unheard-of limits, had already begun to force physicists in general to the consideration of the truth of this or a similar theory. See Signor Storelli, inventor of the Sliding-Arc Water Sphere, in a paper read before the R. I. S. E. M. E., "I personally am convinced that the explanation of the Water-Sphere lies in some kinetic relation, as yet uncharted, between form and energy, per se—the study of which relation and its utilisation will be the next great advance in the Science of Physics!"

a bit bored with it all. He glanced tentatively, even longingly, (and was his glance observed?) in the direction of the engine of death, now shrouded under its black cover. The night was like the hair on his scalp and he began to wish once more to be at his post at the oculascope while the old gentleman sent his bulls-eye bullet piercing the walls of distant chambers and the sleepers therein, of whose multiple respirations his fainting senses were now but the echo, slumbrously receding (and had it been only that this fevered desire for action might be born in the young man's brain that the old gentleman had launched on his astonishing burst of rhodomontade?)

And he was still talking. ". . . simple for our *homo physico-philosophicus!* Form equals Energy—naturally. But first let us ask how far we may safely. . . ." (The room whistled with light but through the window Charles saw the loitering night, beguiling, like a Spanish senorita. He felt sleepy. The air was like knives in his nostrils and). The old gentleman was still talking.

. . . "whole question of invisibility brings us to—

"Conclusion 3: that *Form is but a kind of inorganic blastomere, of which Energy can be considered as the epiblast*"!

"Oh! Quite probably! Quite probably!" Charles Dograr agreed, and then began feverishly taking notes.

"Then, if the biological analogy be sound, which I have, to my own satisfaction at any rate, amply proved in practise, it follows that *Form is actually a kind of static growth through which Energy, by a very real form of metastasis, is derived.*

"Energy then, to put it more simply, is merely isomeric Form. And Form, therefor, is capable of indefinite projection through space—*provided that the co-related energy be entirely endogenous!*

"And now—" the old gentleman produced a large diagram (reproduced herewith; see page 108). Then, going to his machine, he opened the stereopticon-like chamber, revealing an intricately interweaving, oppositely-ascending pair of quartz tubes or cylinders, each of which looked rather like the skeleton of a pyramid, ascending in continuous, diminishing, proportionate rectangles "—for the mechanics of the thing. . . ." (And

Charles [9]

[9] . . . . began thinking heavily. He had enemies, or rather he was enemies for example the man who had bumped in the gray suit and there had been a guard on the Third Avenue El not to mention the waitress at Childs as some possibility in the conception awakened his brain and he stared assiduously at the old gentleman. One had but to ask apparently in the future he must get the addresses. 97 Juniper Street? he asked but he said no and.

(10)

[20] "Look here," he said thickly rising and he waving a sh-h-h hand the old gentleman understanding nodding to the blackdraped engine but with a sly eye:

"Take a few hours rest now."

VIII—"I THINK HE IS LIGHT OF HEART!"

IN a small room on the third floor of the house across the way, a lady removed from her eyes a small pair of binoculars, and laid them on a table.

"It don't look as if they'd do much tonight," she murmured half aloud, and yawned. "But Fred is going to be disappointed." Although she had stopped speaking abruptly, closing her ruby lips and firm white teeth almost sternly over the last word, there was a suspended intonation in her voice which would have moved most authors, in describing the scene, to have affixed, immediately after the letter 'd' in the word 'disappointed,' the following row of dots: '. . . . .'

Since we are now introducing this lady to the attention of the interested reader, some description of herself and the *milieu* in which we find her is perhaps appropriate—though (if we are to consider the word "appropriate" in all its bearings) the lateness of the hour (it was 4:45 A. M.), the intimacy of the chamber (it was her bedroom) and the negligence of her apparel (she wore only a blue silk chemise and blue satin mules) must deter us from carrying too far our investigations.

In fact, had the reader been led actually to open the door of that chamber at the hour mentioned, the first glance about the walls of the room would have led him (if he be as mature in experience as we suppose he is) to close the door softly and make his way out to the street again (if he be as decent and upright a man as we pray him to be).

Arriving, as we have postulated, in the flesh, the first thing to strike the eye of our reader would perhaps have been the bed. It was large, of imposing structure, covered with a pink silk coverlet. At its head a pink-shaded light cast a seductive glow on the pillows. He would have noticed the washstand, with its soap and basin and towels and oilburning water-heater. He would have observed the pages clipped from *La*

Vie Parisienne, Sans Gêne and *La Revue Parisienne* that had been tacked along the wall. He would not have failed to remark the photos, in bathing suit, lingerie and the altogether, of the lady herself. His eye, travelling about the room, must surely have encountered the form of its feminine tenant, but by this time the corybantic wantonness of the setting most have struck some vague but responsive chord in his memory and have driven him from the temple of this modern Cybele, ere her lips had formed the accepted phrase of greeting, "Hello dearie!"

In other words, the lady was a prostitute. In the flesh, the reader must have fled from her—or paid ten dollars to investigate her charms. We see no valid reason why the readers of this book should be otherwise dealt with. On receipt of ten dollars we will forward in plain wrapper a complete and catalogued (illustrated) description of Madame Helène Montmorency.

In the meantime, however, the lady. Drawing one knee—pearl-like, almost translucent in its rounded loveliness—within the circle of her soft white arms, she remained for some time, meditant. Her eyes, dark beneath the flame of her rutile hair; her lips, murmurous with unformed melody; the softened chin; the tremulous volutes of the creaming throat—all, all revealed her dreams to be of someone dear to her.

Who was that someone—the unknown "Fred" she had previously mentioned?

"Put the sheet back over it again all right, anyway,"—she spoke, half at random, to herself. "The kid, too. . . ." Here some unuttered thought made her laugh a moment, gurglingly and low.

Then she was silent again, rocking back and forth in her chair, the white knee still netted in the whiter hands. "But what in the devil can they be up to, anyway? . . . Five o'clock in the morning. . . .

"It certainly beats me!" she concluded, and rose, and yawned. Then, yielding to a sudden impulse, she once more seized the binoculars and directed them at the window of the house across the way.

That impulse was to change the course of many lives, but none to a destiny more bittersweet than her own. For what she saw, as her many-times magnified gaze swept the front of the house, made her start and draw back a moment in alarm—and then, tentatively, as if in response to a signal but half understood and less than half expected, wave an arm in greeting!

Across the dark, deserted slot of Twenty-Third Street, brought close to hers by the magic glass but still veiled by umbriferous night, she saw a face—a young face, but a man's face withal—a face lit with the dignity of desire and beautiful with longing. She saw the face of Charles Dograr, framed in the casement of his chamber window, and the eyes—such eyes as ne'er before had gazed in hers—seemed staring directly at her!

It had been an instant. She could not be sure. But then she had seen the handkerchief floating at the tips of his fingers—had seen him wave it at her. She had started back, a prey to a thousand conflicting emotions. Then, as we have seen, tentatively, even timidly she had waved in return. An instant later, grown bolder, her slender hand had drawn a kiss from her imprisoning lips;

a breath had wafted it to his. And with dilate eyes she saw the kiss, 'mid a sweet swarm of others, returned to her—seemed, even, to feel them hot upon her cheeks and brow, and lips.

She heard the door of her room open behind her!

"That you, Fred?" she queried, summoning all her woman's will to keep the tremor from her voice.

"Who tha hell did yexpect?" came the coarse reply. And now she turned, riant, assured, drawing down the curtain as she looked at him.

"Well, you never can tell, honey, these days," she replied glitteringly.

"Listen!" said the man savagely. He was blond, large, heavily set. He had thrown himself on the bed. "Listen!" And for a moment she thought he would spring at her. But his manner changed, became secretive. His voice fell to a whisper. "*Been watching?*" he queried.

"Yes."

"Well—?"

"Why, it's just like I said, Fred. There's nothing in it."

"Well, what're they doin' over there, then?"

She faced him, riant, insolent. "You want to know, do you? Well, I'll tell you. They're developing photographs!"

The man spat. "Hell!" he ground out. Then, becoming suddenly suspicious: "Well, whassa big machine for, wit ta cloth over it?"

"That's to print the pictures with, silly." She had affected an air of careless impatience as she spoke, but her eyes watched him furtively. His knowledge was wide, she knew. Had he ever printed photographs? Would he detect her subterfuge?

He seemed to believe, to be convinced. But he took up the strain again. "Well, whadda they woika night for?" he wanted to know. "Listen, Helen, the's somethin going on there, take it from me." She shrugged her shoulders, riant, beautiful, and the man's dull brain told him, and his greedy eyes told her that never before had he found her more maddeningly desirable. "It's the nearest thing to a clue, anyway, that I've struck yet, an the whole Headquarters is woikin ona case. Listen, Helen, if I could put ta hooks inta them two grifters they'd jump me to a Captain right off ta shot. Ta chief is damn' near nuts, what witta papers gassin him an all. Listen Helen. . . ."

He had not, as yet, suspected her. She must lead him on. "I don't give a damn, Fred," she said, drawing near to him, "whether you're a captain or not. It's you I want—you—you!"

Something in her tone must have set him on his guard, for he thrust her from him. "Me, hell!" he grated. An evil light came in his eyes. He seized her wrist, twisted it cruelly. She sank to her knees before him, tortured, but riant still. "Listen!" he ground out. "Look at me, damn you! Are you tryin ta double-cross me? What—were—they—doin—over—there? Come across!!"

The agony of it twisted her supple body like fire but she stared straight at his eyes. They were hard blue like manacles on her tortured soul but she thrust them off.

"Photos—oh! God! Fred! That's killing me! Photographs . . . they were developing . . . photographs . . . photo. . . ."

He thrust her from him with an oath.

"Gimme them glasses!" He rushed to the window. Another oath, as he saw the windows dark. A sigh of relief from her, as she noticed that the face of the young man had been withdrawn. Fred slammed the glasses on the table and turned, like silk on steel, to her.

"Listen girlie," he said. "Get this straight. I'm givin ya tha whole dope. I don't say I know, now, but it looks damn funny ta me. These guys sit up all night wrastlin wit ta old Kodak? Mabeso, but every time tey do, why somebody gets moidered somewheres. Now I aint cracked dis yet down to Headquarters. I'm woikin on it alone, see—you an me. If we put it on to dem, it's a stripe for me, see, an a big swell fur coat for you.

"But if you double-cross me," he spat, and stepped closer to her, as she watched him, fascinated. "—if you pitch *me*, girlie—"

His arm flashed out suddenly. There was the smack of a hard fist across a soft cheek, and the lovely form went tumbling to the floor.

He jerked her up. "Don't cry, dearie," he

grinned in mock tenderness. "That ain't tha be-ginnin o what I'll do ta ya!" He held her a mo-ment, staring into her streaming eyes, then shoved her roughly to the bed. She lay limp across the satin coverlet, sobbing.

The man picked up his derby hat and moved to the door. He stood a moment, hand on latch, grinning at her.

"Don't forget now," he grated, in his deadly voice and was gone.

Slowly Helène Montmorency dragged herself to the window, watched Fred stalk up the street. He turned the corner of Ninth Avenue. Dawn was coming. The windows across the way were like fishes' eyes, vacant. Her phantom love had disappeared.

"Oh!" she sobbed. "If he only knew. If only I could tell him! There's danger, and I alone can know of it. I must tell him!" Slowly, as she watched, the tears dried and the smiles came back. Tenderly, she tossed a kiss to that silent upper window, and another, and a third.

"I love him," she breathed. "I think he is light of heart!"

The streets grew brighter, she watching. A new day had dawned, for the sleeping city. And a new day, too, a day of love and hope, and joy and fear and hate, was dawning for Helène Montmorency.

And still she stayed there, breathing kisses and passionate avowals to her mysterious lover, across the dreary wastes of drab old Twenty-Third Street!

IX—INTERLUDE

IT was Sunday and the great office buildings
honeycombs of silence. People were circulat-
ing slowly along the streets of the city except
the protuberant man in a brown suit with his
deprecative spouse walked along paths tremulous
like eggs about to hatch he was rattling his stick
against the rusted black railings; the fountain
plopped and plashed.

Charles Dograr sat in Madison Square Park
like a man in a parachute green-gray-yellow falling reminiscently heavenward his finger between
the pages of his book watching the cane an at-
tenuated focus of all the sun in the air spinning
the man and his wife and his accordeon trousers
toward where the old Garden buzzed treacherously like a longnecked turtle. The circus was
there. Adeline.

A slush of silence waded over the Park after
the passing of a Fifth Avenue bus. To fling to

the moment passing birdly he was fumbling for a dutiful crumb of thought: he had plenty to think about as (glistering like listerine) a page from an old newspaper swished rattling along the path. At an immeasurable distance across Fifth Avenue where (a whirr (the chatter of traffic   GOLDBAUM & BIRNER   enmoiling) of red-   SILKS   yellow axles) winked maliciously into a building-window (through the poignant moment of disparition) as New York again had swooned smotheringly over him (her face drowning) irremediably (into the freckled sides of the Flatiron Building). A barb of premonition transfixed his heart. He got up hastily and walked over to the stage entrance of the Garden.

"I've come to see Miss Adeline Laggick," he announced to the doorman.

"No visitors allowed."

Charles bowed, crossed the street, disguised himself as a Western Union messenger boy and presented himself at the door again.

"Telegram for Miss Adeline Laggick."

"Second tier up, third door from the staircase. It's dressing room number eighteen."

The long arc of the lower corridors was yellowly dim-lighted. Here in like crucibles of shadow the animals: he heard the roof yawn to the growl of a lion, the pad-pad of the tiger's fringed paws. There was a sweet sickening odor crawling up everywhere from the straw; a man was mixing bran in a pail; three or four others among red-painted band-wagons were rastling laughing each other about. The vindictive tail of a panther flipped along the sketched gray bars of a cage as he passed. Seeing the flat loose sides of the beast its heavy forepaws stretched past into darkness again on its incessant promenade. His head, dizzying; like climbing a tree he went up the stairs to the dressing rooms.

He knocked on the door number 18. A seemingly impromptu maid opened. He looked in at a bare room, trunks painted with large white letters, clothes against a wall a mirror a dressing table electric light. "Telegram," he said. (She was seated before the mirror in a smudgy kimono pencilling her lips).

"Oh! Lord! What the devil's up now?" she cried pettishly without turning. "Give me it, Marie." He felt as useless as a gas inspector, standing there in the doorway.

He wanted to see her open the missive. It read (he had stopped along the corridor to scribble it on the telegraph blank he always carried with him):—"Meet me without fail Dyckman Street ferry six o'clock important Cousin Herbert." But she had chucked it unopened into a japanned theatrical makeup box.

She glanced irritably up at him. "Well, and what're you waiting for?"

"Any answer?" he replied like a ventriloquist.

"Oh!" She tore open the envelop. An expression of surprise crossed her visage. She reread the screed. "Where did this come from?"

"Twenty-Second Street station."

She was silent a long time, a half smile (or was it, like the carmine flush that mantled her cheeks, the effect of cosmetics only?) on her lips. She roused herself, turning to him, the kimono, unnoticed, falling half open from her exquisite shoulder as she moved. "No. No answer."

She spoke with the decision of a broker, or a woman in love; then, almost as if she owed an apology to the very messenger boy for the curtness of her response—"He—he gave no address," she added hesitatingly. And—"Marie, give this young man a quarter!"

And as the bare yellow door closed him out again into the corridor, he heard her voice, joyously—"Marie, I shall dance this day as I have never danced before!"

And the maid, cajolingly—"Ah! Madame who dance always wiz ze soch gr-rate charm. . . ."

❖

The pain of the long day was o'er. The sky was red, as with blood. Charles Dograr, like a mother in travail, had given birth to six o'clock, and all the timepieces in the city were bawling. She was on the Dyckman Street ferry with him.

❖

They leaned over the rail watching the tasseled foam was hodding on the riverdrift swirled lazily across their bluff bows plunging. The river leaped under the spur of the sun.

◈

"Look!" she cried letting for a moment her small hand touch his arm and softeningly plump it was and ("Shell-like," he thought and really when you saw the flashing longpointed nails faintly corrugated with streaks of light brandished by the taper tenderly-pinchable fingers, really because) pinkly translucent he thought as if the palm were lined with mother-of-pearl. He had overlooked what she had said.

It had been something about canoes. Smiling a woman's uncommunicative smile she slowly withdrew her hand. Her manner gave undue importance to the gesture, allowing a herringboned section of coatsleeve to stare up again at him startledly, as if it didn't belong there.

"It doesn't matter," he said, like Christ.

"But wouldn't *you*—I don't think you even heard a *word* I said!" she said chidingly smiling.

He smiled shyly and a little fixedly in return

and he was to remember the little scurf of powder dustwhite on the edge of her nose.

❖

But he looked determinedly away from New York—as yet.

❖

The wind had brought her relentlessly against him. One arm was raised to secure her tilting hat. He saw how the movement had raised one slim-pointed breast in its satin sheath and he thought how easily he could slip his shoulder his hooked arm into the crisphaired forkedopen hollow of her armpit bringing the fullblossomed breasts crushingly against his lips and his loins twisted a little. "Not yet! Not yet!" he almost cried. A woman's body is so always immanent. The ferry chocked into the slip. Bells rang. Gears ground. Chains rattled. Starters churred in the stopped motors. The sound of feet volleying in the hollow vault of the ferryhouse.

❖

He looked at the sky with a vague recognition, as if he ought to have remembered it, but didn't.

The Palisades on their right had shut down on them like a welloiled shutter. She was probably thinking of something. But her climbing legs up the rocky path kept him from her thoughts. He had all the pleasure of going to be happy.

Halfway up they paused. It was all green with tree shadows. Officially he put his arm around her and felt her hip lean into his. Through a gap in the branches New York showed her calm riverward face to them, yellow like a sunburnt brow above the blue water. For a moment sensation stopped and he could rest with her; then the sweep of his desire spread again. It was like a gaudy-colored fan between them.

"*Oh!* These *bri*ars," she exclaimed, snatching with an annoyed laugh at her short skirt. They were at the top. With no roof of trees over him, naked-headed under the sky, nevertheless he found himself kneeling beside the silk of her knees to disengage the caught hem. They were so close with their soft curves bubblelike lifting upward into the satin-scented tent of her skirt; he saw the grain of the stocking's weave he was so close: an infinity of minute sparkles like dew following the intertwining shining thread and rounding tighter over the creamy calf. Nothing had ever been sweeter in his eye than that curve and (he could touch it. Yes) feeling his hand cupping to the (slide so easily: up: up to the perfumed salacious taut-tendoned pit back of the knee where: all passions rise and: up where the flesh is firm and warm and (in the river below were prows plunging the soft unresistant water lasciviously creaming back and under from the blunt urging and) his arm hook-elbowed sliding resistlessly up to the groove-muscled thighs (if his lips now?) as "Do you roll your stockings?") he was asking fatuously but he wanted the acquiescence of her voice.

It is not a deed for silence and he looked up at her face bent down over the oh! pregnable bastions of her breasts.

"*Ev*erybody does, *sil*ly!" her voice not as it should was saying. She swept her skirt aside with two hands so that it arced across where (childishly it seemed) bare and tightened waterly over the slope of the thighs.

A dawning maliciousness he read on her face;

her eyes were dark with tyrannous expectation.
The moment was mal à propos but:

(Without more ado he had clutched and like
corseting between his two thumbs the flesh inside her leg yielded up to his lips: he kissed.
Something swelled and liberated within him.
From now on a little blood-clot would be like a
machine: so soft the flesh so indecently soft in
its cushioning elasticity that he could bite now
to the bone to find some stiffness meeting his:
in its cleaving depths he could let his jaws clinch
together (and releasing watch the sudden white
and the following flowing red that would wave
into the bluish hollowed teeth-marks under the
film wet from his withdrawing mouth) and:

"*Now* you're being *naugh*ty!" she had said
but a gloze of red (as if rending across his eyes)
before the unstable whiteness of her skin. He put
his arms around her knees and tightened to
weaken her columnar uprightness as one might
uproot a monument but:

"*No!* you're *hurt*ing me!" with the other
arm (but her hand had (caught his arm: he)
stared at her face without seeing: it was not yet

time but) awkwardly. "I *told* you to *stop!*" she had cried and, "I wouldn't have *come* here with you if I'd thought you were going to act like *that!*"

But:

❖

And:

❖

Then:

❖

Afterwards and all that had flowed away and they were sitting on some coarse crisp yellow grass on the edge of the rock. The valley came up at their eyes like a rush of air. There was an as it seemed specially provided dusk and a slow-motion Albany steamer amid a diagram of ripples was headed interminably upstream. It *is* brow-like. As when (slowly) in darkness one comes to perceive the objects about him (but this darkness that we know redshot and dancingly as the woman Time jogs on her elbow) he discovered himself lying on his back with (she was lying beside him smiling) New York shiningly like a brushstroke long yellow across the lower sky.

❖

She was satisfied but he felt her to be an intrusion but her legs crooked about his consciousness.

❖

He thought of the Old Gentleman. Murder, like the villain in the piece, he dragged a little theatrically across his mind. It was only to give a semblance of importance to his complete comfortableness. Besides, somewhere in that shuttling strip of (picked out with purple) yellow an unknow man 3 millimetres tall sat in his window looking out at the Palisades and:

❖

"What shall I *call* you you are not Cousin Herbert of *course* you know I know *that?*"

❖

"Your eyes are like Lake Geneva deep at their bottom is a floor of ice in their cooling blueness my red thoughts are refreshed I would wound you."

❖

"Your eyes are like the daisies of the field you see thousandly and your breasts on their red-blue hubs are as two white chariot wheels that roll me beneath your body."

❖

"Your breasts are like the prows of two pink ships that plunge creaming into my heart's center."

❖

"It's *beau*tiful here isn't it *I'll* tell what we'll come here some *night* and I'll do my *dance* for you!"

❖

"Your shoulders cape about me like the flower of Isis their fragrance shuts out light and darkness through the coiled channels of your navel I shall blow kisses to your heart."

❖

"Your navel is the pin-pricked center whence your beauty is the radius of my world your hips

I see faint with many colors are the ovate cup of my desire."

◈

"Your hips are as a vase my glory my pride my courage shall find root and flourish there."

◈

"I think men are so *silly* they always want to *argue* about something and even when it's about me I find it *tire*some but I love you but I could *hurt* you."

◈

But and both talking neither hearing the other a man had appeared behind them a man black against the sky and from his pose the tapping stick one saw he was blind and deaf and voiceless. Neither saw him. He stood outlined black against the sky. "Death is a complete quiescence," thought McDowell and, "Man, no more than a tree, a stone, shall ever suffer death, save in part, and glancingly. After vomiting, for instance. Not unwisely, in an earlier day, did they speak of men vomiting forth their souls. And the more intimate ejaculations as well. So the seed of life is death and of death, life. X within O—that is the symbol of the universe." And:

❖

"Your hips are like the soil of Heaven your legs like the branching of two white rivers enclose the island of my paradise."

❖

(Sometimes (I think it was I who sat there on the Palisades and lying beside me that wide-cheeked soft-lipped deep-eyed loose-bodied slut waiting smiling for my (or for his) caresses and) sometimes) Charles Dograr: thrillingly and afar he had for a moment heard the march of Life about him (or was it the tapping stick McDowell?) and with a sense of infinite foreboding he had (as you (or I) sitting here in our orchestra chairs (suppose you or I) were to rise and step forward to the scene taking the place of the hero?) Charles in a mood of deep profundity: "I shall not live long," he had said: "in no one of my dreams can I see myself old I shall not live long not more than 250 pages": he had said and (suddenly (dazzledly) as one rising from (is it the

Seine this long blue laughing?) from the water's depth into shattering sunlight he (thrusting up through the perfume of some unknown woman's hair her body sweeter far than he) found himself) sitting there and:

◈

Imperceptibly the Night brooding from the trees (the Night) kneading the white woman's body graying into the gray receiving earth and:

◈

"Death encases Life," and McDowell and: "Man loves not so much with the desire to be a father as to be a grandfather. We progress in alternate interlacing loops, the body the adumbration of the sequitive sperm. Life is an entail on the estate of Death," and:

◈

The blue the (drifting he knew it was Sunday and) "Adeline! Adeline!" he cried frenziedly. She raised her head to stare at him. "This is the last time! My youth is passing. This is the last time! The last time!" and:

◈

McDowell had stepped unperceived (and touching his tapping stick her breasts her body her belly) and:

◈

"*I* was not *made* for finality I'll wear my *white* dress when we come ag*ain,* and:

◈

"The last time! This is the last time!" and (bloating before (his eyes rent apart) the white the (he stared a moment down to the twisting membranous structure) and then: "This is the last time!") it was (he saw distinctly) a fountain blue-white shot from the wound: rose quivering. It sprayed out across the sky. The drops fell: becoming petals; becoming plunging flames: canopied down on her. He was (sprawling on four legs like an animal) regarding nothing.

McDowell had gone on. His stick tap-tapping

receded among the cliffs. Charles Dograr saw nothing. There was a flash of satiny white among the trees.

"Adeline! Adeline!" he called into blankness. He rose and fled.

She heard his footsteps tumbling away among the rocks. A dark stranger came and stood by her side.

X—EIGHTEEN MEN

IT was in Stockholm that I met Fernand Leger, and under rather amusing circumstances. I was strolling one morning on the *Bradgvur,* that most charming of all promenades, when a small man, with narrow head and lank black hair, approached me. I saw at once that it was Leger, and assumed that he, though we had never met, had also recognized me.

" 'He accosted me, and without any prelude, demanded, "Are you a philistine?"

" 'It will perhaps be understood that I did not 'catch on' at once. He was evidently quite terribly in earnest—so much at least was clear.

" ' "Why—why—" I stuttered, when he cut in abruptly: "Well come up to my studio and take a look at my cat. I'm afraid it will die!"

" 'Naturally I went—not to see the cat, but to see his pictures, and was amply rewarded. As it turned out, of course, the explanation was simple, as all explanations are. In his excitement, coupled with his lack of facility in the Swedish tongue, he had confused the word for philistine —'*sturvagsdt*,' with, '*stavgardt*,' meaning veterinary!

" 'Nevertheless,—as Leger himself admitted when I laughingly taxed him with it—the incident has to me always seemed a strikingly just epitome of his artistic principles. . . .' "

There was a long vague pause for fumbling among the leaves. "M-m-m-m., . . . ah!" and—

" '. . . was his terse and nervous prose, and his astonishing gift of mother-wit, rather than any social graces, that procured Max Beerbohm his invitation to the *soirée* at the d'Alençons, for he had an unpleasant tendency toward kleptomania that made his friends a little uneasy in his. . . .' "

"Here!" said Charles. "Let me read it myself."

Asa Huddleberry, filled with a bulbous delight, handed over the manuscript. He was a critic on the Bookman, or was it the Atlantic Monthly?

"What do you think of the title?" he demanded. " 'From A Critic's Diary'—eh?"

Charles looked up to find the man's large, flaccidly intense eyes swelling at him. He laid the bulky sheaf on the floor. "Oh. . . ." he said.

I have remarked that sometimes I think it was I who sat one rose-scented evening on the Palisades beside the girl Adeline and indeed in many ways this Charles Dograr was very like myself.

He was awkwardly conscious of people. He felt ticklishly their glances. He was lumberingly docile at times and at times fanatically precise.

His morals, his ethics, his philosophy had not as yet sharply emerged for his mind was still clouded by strange, voluminously sweeping ideas of which his most tenaciously revered was a belief that the operation of the world's forces on him would combine in his own preservation and advancement. He had abiding faith in his own ability and in what we (but he never) would call his luck. And he forced himself almost consciously to strengthen that faith, with a vague sense that if he could make it strong enough not even Fate would have the heart to disabuse him of it.

This childish tendency to animate the inanimate—to motivate the immutable—to render scrutative the inscrutable—was everywhere characteristic of him. If people seemed poignantly alive to him, objects and even objectives were more than alive. Four thousand years ago he would have been a priest of Isis; and now not a packing-box, not a cobblestone of the roadway, still less the Force that made his ambiance, but was endowed, in his philosophy, with Mind and Will.

The effort of his logic was to discover, not the reason, but the reasoning of Things.

Nevertheless, the murder of Edward Trulge, coupled with the two or three that swiftly followed (into collusion in which he had been so cleverly tricked by the old gentleman) had disturbed him greatly. But now he was sitting in Asa Huddleberry's studio in the rooming house, listening with marcescent interest to the other's volubility.

"I should like," Huddleberry was saying, "I

should like to write a detective story—a mystery story. . . . But one in which no one should know what crime had been committed—nor who had committed it. . . ."

"That's true of all crimes, isn't it, rather?" asked Charles and watched himself inject a careless laugh, like a hypodermic, into the man's mind. But:

"No one. . . . There should be a dream quality about it all. . . ." His eye lighted; a rising enthusiasm informed his customarily level tones and he waved his long thin hands in wider gestures—"A dream quality, yes; a brooding sense of Something—no one quite knowing what—but Something dread, and menacing, and terrible. A Something that sets all the boasted power of civilization at naught—," he raised his hand as Charles gave evidence of being about to speak, "—at naught, and mocks the puny strength of men. . . ."

"After all," murmured Charles comfortingly to himself, "how puny the little things really are. I *do* get foolish about them." He looked with renewed lightheartedness at Huddleberry, lying

there on the crimson chaise longue, the thin figure of him wrapped in his purple dressing gown,
and almost took out his pencil and note book
like a reporter, as the man went on.

"It shall be my greatest work, that. I see them
now in my mind's eye, my characters as I shall
write them—small, busy important silhouettes
against the black shadow of Fate. . . . They
move about, fussily occupied with their lilliputian
affairs—beautiful fragile women . . . men
evanescently powerful in the affairs of nations
themselves soon—ah! soon to crumble into the
forgetting dust. . . . Men, women. . . ."

"Don't you think," cut in Charles, forgetting
he was interrupting, for a new idea had struck
him, "we often confuse permanency with importance in a curiously illogical way? Isn't it
often the very impermanence of the thing which
makes its importance?

"Man lives his slender span and dies—and it is
just that his span is short which gives his death
real importance. That's why fresh strawberries
are important. A hundred years' erosion crum-
bles a tower, and so does a thunderbolt—in half

a second—and therein lies the importance of the thunderbolt. How unimportant man would be, if he lived a thousand years!

"But still. . . . A telegraph pole, for instance. . . . No. . . . And yet . . ." He relapsed a moment, and the Great Critic, seizing the occasion, went on:

"Men, women, statesmen, courtesans, plotters. . . . and yet, in the mind of each the dread questions are constantly impending—'What is it that threatens?'—'And for whom?'—'If Death, then who shall be the victim?'—'Who the murderer?'—'Where the scene of the tragedy?'—'Shall it be I who will strike the fatal blow?'—'Or shall I receive it?' . . ."

He paused again, staring dramatically at the corner of the ceiling. "And the end—dramatic, inevitable, but veiled in mystery. . . . 'Was there a murder?'—'Who was the victim?'—they shall ask, my characters. And as each sinks shudderingly to sleep—'Was it I who killed, last night as I thought I slept?'—'Am I, even now, am I dead?' . . . Ah! Yes! It shall be my greatest work, that. It would go well in the American Mercury, don't you think? [1]

Charles, who had been chewing his underlip this while in a meditative frenzy, now sprang suddenly to speech. "No. . . ." he cried. "Don't you see? As I said, a telegraph pole is permanent. If anything *could* make a man important, it is his impermanence. And it does, among his fellows. You carry a basket of eggs more carefully —but not because they are more important— than a basket of potatoes. The eggs, however, seeing themselves cushioned with straw and handled gently, are likely to get pretty pompous about it. So with ourselves. Man's great fragility, and the consequent delicacy necessary in handling a human being lest one inadvertently destroy him, lead us—though quite fallaciously—to consider him very important indeed. But it is when man tries to struggle with true permanence that he becomes ridiculous. Even in small things—as dozens of people have pointed out. For instance: every locomotive that is built means that all men die a little. Do you see what I mean?"

[1] Var. 1915 ed. ". . . in the *Smart Set*, don't you think?"
Var. 1959 ed. ". . . in *Partisan Review*, don't you think?"

He looked up hopefully. The afternoon trembled. Huddlebery was frowning.

"What," he asked, "has all this about locomotives got to do with my story?"

"Oh!" Charles re-collected himself, as after a leap. "The story. . . . Murder, wasn't it? I think there are only two people who could write a murder story—the murderer and the victim. For example," he had risen and was at the door, "suppose I were to commit a murder tonight, I would probably then be able to write a good story—from the standpoint of the murdered. If I murdered you, then you would be in the best possible position to write from the standpoint of the murderer."

"Oh! Well," Huddleberry commented petulantly. "If you will try to be clever. . . ."

"Not at all!" Charles himself had been frightened by the sudden firmness of voice as he had pronounced the words. Huddleberry, however, had not observed. He went away relieved, dragging the bloody word behind him.

That night, however, after the switch had been closed for the eighth time, and Charles still was fiddling with the adjustor-screws, the old gentleman remonstrated mildly.

"Not that I mind," he explained, "only the continued drain on the current might cause comment. That light-box uses a powerful lot of juice. What is it, my boy?"

"Do you know the address of the New Republic?" asked Charles. "I've already been through the Atlantic, Nation, Aesthete, Dial and Vanity Fair. The man I'm looking for I don't know where he hangs out."

The old gentleman cast a sly grin downward. "Your literary friend?"

"There are seven incentives to murder," Charles replied. "So far I've tried three: curiosity, sex-fatigue, and boredom." He patted the focal barrel with comforted eyes. "What's up tonight?" he asked.

The old gentleman opened a brief-case containing maps, diagrams, key-molds, etc. "Well," he began. "I think we'd better rehearse the City Mercantile Bank affair. . . ."

"How many?"

"Eighteen men. The night watchman, four

special police, the driver and two guards of the armored car, the teller and assistant teller of the bank, the agent of the Burgeson, Rich Company, our two grifters and the driver of the car I've engaged. . . ." The old gentleman paused, smiling softly up at Charles. "It's always better to get rid of one's accomplices, don't you think?"

Charles nodded grimly. "That makes only fourteen," he commented.

The old gentleman waved a hand. "Well, and the usual number of innocent bystanders," he explained. Charles nodded comprehension.

"Eighteen. . . ." he murmured.

They were silent a moment. A moment, compassion sat heavy on the withers of Charles Dograr's pride. His jaws flattened with pity. The old gentleman observed, and his gaze fell, like a caress from his crooked old fingers, on the wavy locks of our hero's careless head and internally he gave unctuous approval. Then Charles was brusk again.

"I noticed the car downstairs."

"The Hispano—yes."

"Fast work then—eh?"

"It may be. I thought we'd better be sure. It means nineteen millions."

Charles leaned back in his chair. "In gold?"

"Gold coin."

"What time?"

"The armored car with the shipment comes to the bank at exactly midnight."

"Tomorrow?"

"Yes."

There was silence. The heavy yellow brilliance of the room showered like whispering gold on the two. "Nineteen millions. . . ."

"That's enough for a while, eh?" urged the old gentleman. His eye grew suddenly waterily piteously beseeching.

"We might go away for a time. . . . eh, Charles? With nineteen millions. We'll buy a yacht, what do you say, Charles? I saw the very thing in the harbor yesterday, coming in from Long Island. . . . Gibraltar . . . the Mediterranean. . . . Monaco. . . . Suez. How would you like that, Charles? With your old partner. . . . Alone. . . . Ah! . . ." He had flopped forward on the floor.

On his knees on the floor before Charles amazed, and clutching for his hand like an old woman in a Victorian novel. "Just we two, Charles. Alone there . . . on the blue water. I have dreamed of it! I have longed for it—haven't you seen?—since that first night when we—murdered that man out in Union Hill—we, together.

"Must I confess? He was the first . . . the first time I had ever raised my hand to kill! It was your young fiery energy that nerved me to it!" He gave way to a fit of throaty laughter. Charles felt his thighs prickle into gooseflesh. "But that night—that night, I could have dipped my hands into his warm blood—dipped it up with my two hands and blessed you with it, to consecrate our love. Charles, do you hear? Our love!"

His eyes glared wildly. Charles, drawn back deep in his chair, saw them as a man, alone on a narrow road at night, sees the headlights of a motorcar approaching swiftly, roaring.

And the old gentleman's voice went on, the words coming hoarsely as if some hot inner blast were forcing them through the taut channels of his throat. "You know—you must know that I love you! My money! The ardor of my soul! The pride of my intellect! I throw them all at your feet! Charles! . . . (There was an air of theatricality about it all. Mae West in a more advanced moment might have done the scene. Charles waited). . . . Charles! Ah! Charles! We shall defy them all! We will shrivel their brains! Like burnt walnuts! And blood! Blood! Blood!"

He was scrambling to his feet now, his hand crawling toward the boy's planed face.

But Charles now (the moment of horror passed) could almost have laughed, in fact did—insofar as a twisted contortion of the lips, a flaring release of the tensed facial muscles can be called laughter.

He saw with a cold skilled eye the sweat that stood on the old gentleman's forehead, saw the sagging, chattering, lecherous mouth.

And still—"Nineteen millions! It shall be yours and nineteen more, and ninety more as well . . . and all the wealth of Ind. . . . All the jewels of Araby! All, all yours . . . if you but say one word—one word! Ah! Charles! Speak! Speak! . . ."

Charles for a moment sat on the top of the world as (with a decided gesture) like a man putting out a candle he extinguished all emotion, pushing the old gentleman pivotting away.

"What nonsense!" he rasped. And, with the naked assurance of youth, "How about this City Mercantile Bank? Let's stick to business."

The moment that followed must be allowed to weigh with centuries. Man is the toy of Fate, but the emotion within him is like the gravity wheel that, once whirling, propels the child's locomotive up impossible slopes. Arrested, in the one case it crumples the painted plaything—in the other it disrupts the mind and all the plans of men. During that moment the old gentleman had turned his head away, moving his hands across his features like a quick-change artist preparing for the next act.

Then his head rotated .on his wrinkled neck. He was seen to be smiling.

"Ah! yes!"—but his voice came gaspingly—

"The eighteen men!" (But, "Nineteen!" a de-moniac whispering in his brain.)

"That's better!" approved Charles, uncom-prehending.

"We'll rehearse tonight."

"How about the three grifters? They all here?"

"In the next room——" Each word had been like clicking a camera shutter. Now his voice broke. And——"Ah! Charles!" once again he was pleading. "The world shall ring with our names, if you but speak. . . . Dograr—sweet sound! —and Picrolas; indivisibly joined to the fat world's horror. . . . Dograr and Picrolas! . . . Picro. . . ."

"Picrolas!" The boy's voice blanched. "Picro-las!!" And the air in the silent room rang like the lip of a bell at the fated syllables and fear ran down through the boy's belly like a skewer through butter. "Picrolas! You—are—Picrolas?"

The old gentleman's face before him was like a knot of green and yellow yarn, untwisting. But the mouth preserved its deadly, even smile.

"You know. . . . You have heard . . . of Picrolas?"

The voice came to him distantly; the smile poniarded his vision. Who—who living had not heard and, hearing, feared the dread name? Who, as the arch-fiend's tale of crime and desolation had unrolled before the eyes of a startled world, had not felt his eyes grow hot with tears—his heart cold with shame that humanity could harbor so deadly a viper. Men, hearing his iniquities, had sworn that no mother surely, but some devil must have borne him. Frail women's hair had grown white in a single night, simply at reading a newspaper account (and one no doubt censored) of but one of his misdeeds.

Picrolas! Charles felt his courage shrivel now. He shuddered, and the man's grinning face loomed evilly before him.

Two months they had been together now and their crimes had been many and foul enough, as they wielded the x-ray bullet.

But it had been (or Charles had thought it so) lighthearted and young. He had quieted his soul —the old, old story!—with a list of his misfortunes, with a tale of the world's misdeeds. He pictured himself a latter-day cavalier, a modern

Robin Hood, astride the machine as the others bestrode their horses. He had told himself that he had robbed the rich to feed the poor. He had—ah! now, with a sickened courage he looked back at it all; he knew now the hideous brain that had urged him on; he saw himself for the fool that he had been.

"Picrolas!"

The old gentleman's smile took on a metallic brilliance. "You—fear—Picrolas?" he asked softly.

The boy was beyond words.

"Say but one word. . . ." the voice came softly, cajolingly, "One word, and you need not fear him." Under it all was the grimace.

"No! No! Come what will I—" Charles Dograr had risen to his feet. The old gentleman's hand halted him.

"Sh-h-h-h!"

Someone was knocking gently at the door. A moment, when both stared at the other. Then Charles Dograr rose, strode across the room. Anything was better than this inactivity! He opened. Three faces emerged in the gloom—the faces of men steeped in vice, hardened in crime.

They were the three accomplices of the multiple murder the old gentleman had planned for the morrow night.

At another time, Charles would have smiled with mocking courage at their twisted lips, glittering eyes and cut-throat visages—would have vaunted himself for the power he held over them and their ilk.

Now, he could hardly keep countenance before them, for the shame that clamored at his heart. One spoke:

"Whinever yeze arre ready sorr, thin we do be surely," he announced in his laughable Irish brogue. It was a burly, broken-nosed ruffian.

Another, dark, thin, venomous, concurred. "Sure, Let's get-a da woik done. It be much-a late-a." One saw he was of Italian origin.

"Come in, gentlemen." The old gentleman welcomed them with ironic courtesy, but his eye bored ever at Charles. "Sit down."

And then (perhaps God, looking down, may have (no other, in the sleeping city, could have) seen in that lit room) three brutish men and a brown-haired, fair-faced boy, coached and guided by a wry-eyed old gentleman, went through the preparations for a great crime.

It might have been a game they played, for all evidence to the casual eye (if the casual eye could have overlooked the grim, set faces of the participants, and the anxious instructions of the old gentleman).

First, maps appeared. All the possibilities of the locality were canvassed—even, with chairs and desk and cushions, a miniature map of the scene was made. Then, down to the smallest detail, the part that each man was to play was memorized, the old gentleman supervising. And strange it was to see these blackguards, as each his turn devolved, rise like schoolchildren to recite his lesson. There was much they did not understand.

"Sure, I get-a you. I drives around-a tha corner and-a—"

"No! Not around it. Drive to the corner and stop there!" corrected the old gentleman. "In that way you block both approaches."

"All-a right-a," the Italian assented, it seemed to Charles with an ill grace. "I drive to tha corner-a. An' I jumps out wit me gun."

"Only don't worry about your gun," advised the old gentleman impatiently. The ruffian stared.

"You said-a dey was eighteen o' dem!"

"That'll all be taken care of." Proudly, Picrolas patted the barrel of the x-ray gun. "I will take care of that."

"You? But yez said, sorr, that yez wouldn't be there surely."

"I won't." The men looked bewilderedly at each other. Charles smiled. The old gentleman turned to him and for a moment their glances met in the old derisive camaraderie.

Then Charles hardened and he turned away. But, for a long time, the old gentleman's eye, unnoticed, was pinned to the young man's face.

Charles had been thinking he noticed something that recollected the face of one of the men to his mind. The man wore a derby hat.

"Haven't I seen you somewhere?" he asked. It was a burly, swaggering fellow.

"Me?" The man pictured surprise. "Naw. I just got in from Niagara Falls today."

"Oh?" Charles thought little more of it. And yet, in the back of his brain as, glibly, he ran through the recital of his part of the crime's consummation, there lingered a faint, evasive memory. A blonde man . . . with a derby hat . . . he had walked in fear . . . of what? . . . one early morning. . . .

"You were never in New York before?"

The fellow shook his head negatively.

Half an hour later, the old gentleman professed himself satisfied with the rehearsal and dismissed them.

"Till tomorrow!" Then he turned to Charles. "Do not go, Charles. One word before . . ."

Bruskly, Charles tore his sleeve from the man's grasp; he spoke not a word in reply, but signalled ahead to the man in the derby hat.

"Wait a minute there," he called. "I'll walk down with you."

Left alone, the old gentleman walked heavily across the room until he stumbled almost blindly against the mechanism of the x-ray rifle. He laid his head between his arms on the polished surface. For a time, he wept. Then, suddenly, he raised his head again and his face was horrible to behold. And he raised his clenched hands to Heaven, and his voice came choked with passion.

"Fool!" he gasped. "Twice—triple accursed fool! You spurn me—me, Picrolas! Ha! Ha! You fool, know you not that the power still rests here—with me? Nineteen shall die tomorrow! Nineteen! Here—I swear it! Yourself—you have sealed your doom! Tomorrow's sun shall be your last, or Picrolas is forsworn!"

(a) Mr. Rupert Pragman put the bottle of milk under his left arm and opened the door with his right. Hurriedly he entered the house. His wife was standing impatiently in the diningroom. —"Hurry up and sit down to your dinner. The nice tunafish on toast I made that you like'll be all cold," she said.—"Did anybody come while I was away?" asked Mr. Pragman.—"No. I think that detective stuff of yours is all a fake," she said. "Sit down to the table," she added.— "Well, all right," Mr. Pragman agreed. They sat down and ate the tunafish on toast.—"It certainly was pretty good," said Mr. Pragman afterward.

(b) "Well, let's see what we can get on the radio," suggested Mr. Pragman to his wife.—"All right, Rupert," said she. Just then there was a knock on the door.—"You go see who it is," said Mr. Pragman.—"No. It's your turn," said his wife. He opened the door. A stranger stood on the doorstep. Summoning up all his courage, Mr. Pragman proposed, "EGGS ARE INDETERMINATE BUT FOWLS ARE FIRM." The stranger bowed. He was a distinguished-looking foreigner.[1] He spoke with a slight accent.[2] "IF MOSCOW REVERSES SELL AT ONCE!"—"Come in," said Mr. Pragman.—"We have no time to lose," said the stranger.—"Just a minute till I get my hat," said Mr. Pragman. He got his hat. They went out together. Mrs. Pragman, when left alone, sat down by the radio. She began fiddling with the dials. Two minutes later the machine shuddered and burst into flames. At the same time a heavy brilliance scalloped her brains. The poor woman was dead.[3]

[1] This, the astute reader need hardly be reminded, was undoubtedly a disguise.

[2] The assumption of a foreign accent is a familiar device among detectives, having for object the deception of their prey. In this they attain at times to a high degree of proficiency.

[3] Was this caused by some as yet uncomprehended combustive capacity inherent in the construction of the radio? Or was it a magnetic diffraction of the rays of the x-ray bullet as the old gentleman, even then, searched for the brain of Charles Dograr? The details, though scanty, of the good lady's death would perhaps render the latter hypothesis more probable.

(c) Pragman and the stranger got onto the Subway.—"I suppose you're from Foster R. Foster," asked Pragman timidly.—"Ssh! That is not his real name," said the stranger. "His real name is Charles Dograr!" [4]—"He told me he was working on the Trulge Murder Case," said Pragman.—"He was," said the stranger.[5]—"Well, I thought as much," said Pragman.—"We have got to go to Chicago," said the stranger. They got off at the Grand Central and bought two tickets to Chicago. As there happened to be a train leaving they got on and went to Chicago.

(d) "Come in here," said the stranger, pausing before a pawnshop when they had got to Chicago. They went in and the stranger bought a little gilt locket. They went out in the street again and opened it. In the back was a picture of

[4] This is astonishing! Obviously, someone has been working on the Trulge case without the concurrence, perhaps even without the knowledge, of the author. The complete ignorance on the part of Mr. Coates of the most elementary principles of plot construction, apparent throughout the book, is here devastatingly revealed. The reader, left to his own devices in identifying the stranger, will perhaps do well to assume that it is none other than the missing Herbert Trask. Thus the introduction of a new character is avoided at so late a moment.

[5] Sic!

a little, fair-haired girl. The stranger looked at it for some time. "We must hurry," said he at last. They turned down a side street.

(e) Toward the end of Halstead Street, somebody shot at them from an upper window. The stranger preserved his sang-froid.—"Take the number of that house," he said. Pragman took the number down in a little notebook he always carried. The stranger paused at an ashcan. He pulled out a worn old broom. With a magnifying glass he studied the handle. Then he went to a drugstore and bought some bichloride tablets. —"These are a deadly poison," he said, showing them to Pragman and smiling mysteriously.— "Oh! Are they?" asked Pragman.—"Let us go in and buy a couple dozen bananas," said the stranger. "We have long a journey before us." They went in and bought the bananas. Coming out of the store, a dark-bearded man ran past them and disappeared in an apartment house, crying: "Eighteen men! Eighteen men!" It was only one of the curious events of the day.

(f) Dawn found them in Erie, Pennsylvania. The stranger told Pragman to wait a minute while he went into a grocery store. Pragman waited and the stranger went into the grocery store. He conversed for a long time with the proprietor. When he came out he had a can of tomatoes and looked pleased.—"I had to buy these tomatoes so as he wouldn't get suspicious," he explained. "But I found out the man we are after is an old fellow, very mathematical, and he deserted his wife six years ago in this town. What will we do with this can of tomatoes?"—"Eat them?" asked Pragman.—"What we better do, we better go see this man's wife. She lives right around the corner," said the stranger. "Have you got the number of that house in Chicago?" he added.—"No 436," replied Pragman.—"It's the same number. Wait here till I get the morning editions," said the stranger. They were full of all the details about the Nine Prominent Critics Die By X-Ray Bullet, and it went on to relate how reason shuddered when the city waked up today to find that such men as Harry Hansen, William Soskin, Heywood Broun, Bruce

Gould, Waldo Frank, Henry Seidl Canby, Asa Huddleberry and James Thurber and George Jean Nathan were made the victims of a dastardly attack late last night and the police were hopelessly at sea because no motive could be imagined for the murders unless by the Communists from Moscow. The stranger looked worried. Then his brow cleared.—"Well, anyway, Adeline is safe," he muttered.[6]—"Do we go see the wife?" queried Pragman.—"No. We have to hurry back to New York. I have got to report to the Chief," said the stranger. "You come along too."

(g) When they got to the station they found the next train was an hour late. They sat in the waiting room to wait for it. "What do you say we eat that can of tomatoes?" asked Pragman. —"Oh! What the hell do I want with the damned tomatoes?" asked the other.—"Well, I will eat them if you don't want them," said Pragman.— "No, you won't either," said the stranger. So

---

[6] This dissipates all uncertainty as to the identity of the stranger. It is indubitably Herbert Trask. He, too, is probably in love with Adeline.

saying, he drew his arm back and flung the can of tomatoes away from him. Unfortunately, or fortunately as events later turned out, the can smashed through a window in the waiting room and landed in the face of a man who, unknown to them, had been regarding them all along. There was a great uproar at this. Pragman and the stranger rushed outside to see what was the matter.

(h) When they got outside, the Station Master was helping the man who had been hit to his feet. When he saw them he rushed up to them.— "Get out of here," he cried angrily. "You pretty near broke the face off of our Superintendent of Schools."—"No, we won't get out. We have got our tickets," asserted Pragman. The Station Master was about to commence an angry retort, when the stranger, who had been closely regarding the supposed Superintendent of Schools, rushed over to his side.—"So he calls himself the Superintendent of Schools, does he?" he asked sarcastically. "Well, us detectives know him as Denver Mike!" And without more ado he pulled off the false beard off the trembling culprit's face and revealed him in his true colors.

(i) When the man had been put into the patrol wagon and driven off, the stranger turned to Pragman.—"This changes everything," he confided. "This guy Mike is mixed up in the Trulge case too and I have been looking for him a long time and now that I found him I better stay here and give him the Third Degree. Now you go on to New York and deliver this report to the Chief." So saying, he handed Pragman the report.—"What will I do after that?" asked Pragman.—"Well, you better go home and wait there," said the stranger.—"All right," agreed Pragman. But just as he was going to get on the train, the stranger came running after him.—"Wait a minute," he said. "Go to this address and take a room there and watch what happens. Use the name of Edward Sykes. I will come back there tomorrow." So Pragman got on the train. When he had found a seat, for the train was moderately crowded, he looked at the piece of paper where the address was written. It was on West

Twenty-Third Street and more mysterious still if the number of the house could be revealed it would be found to be the same place where Charles Dograr and the old gentleman were now living!

XII—TANGLED TRAILS

When the Bat breaks prison Bill Lawson begins a long chase with a strange ally.

Peter Gerringer sees a man skulking around an empty house. Inside he finds another man and volunteers to help if there is danger. The man leaves him in a locked room and fails to return. Gerringer finds a murdered Chinaman in the next room and his own hat and stick smeared with blood. Another Chinaman appears and proves to be the brother of the dead Chinaman. Gerringer and the Chinaman chase the murderer in Gerringer's car. Bill Lawson is found in an alley in a semi-comatose condition. The mark of a spider has been burned on his forehead. All three give chase. Gerringer is pursued by another car. Gerringer shot and car ditched, one Chinaman killed. While dying tells Gerringer murderer is a man named Clay. Sir Reginald McCloskey's country place in Barsetshire is broken open and robbed. Peter Graham on liner bound for Shanghai becomes acquainted with Moore and daughter Wanda. Also German named Schœnberg. Moore is invalid with weak heart. Moore quarrels with Schœnberg and dies. Matty Josephson is seen at Monte Carlo, clad in rags but playing for huge stakes at chemin de fer. News arrives that the mysterious Isma is at the head of a great Bolshevist plot in Philadelphia, Pa. Wakes at night and finds man in room.

Graham stepped forward.

"What are you doing here?" he demanded, a grim menace in his lowered voice.

Up over the edge of the box slid a tiny, inquisitive head. It was followed by the sinuous body of a little yellow snake.

The Hindu hesitated an instant, read death in Graham's blazing eye, and nodded slowly.

"Kill it then—"

"Honorable sir—"

"Kill it, d—n you!" Graham blazed at him. He jabbed the revolver forward.

As he passed, Graham touched him on the arm. "And tell the man who sent you," he added, "that I am going to get him for this—and for other things."

A few hours later Gerringer glanced at his watch and rose to his feet. Nowhere in the shifting, glittering throng had he been able to catch a glimpse of Wanda Moore. Graham threw down the paper and addressed himself to the dishes his waiter was setting before him, ruminating over the business as he ate.

Like most men gifted with the finer kind of (But the Giverny air is the spawn of silence as: the night dripping dropping on her senses (the mill for example) and like a moonlit ripple curling in the wake of the schooner Night, drifting a nightingale.

One by one she lay there a long time, awaiting: a high branch of lilac was climbing the balcony (but) swaying there (rustling) interrupting: the Singeaut's dogs far away barking; and the mill throbbing so soft it might be thunder in Constantinople. She dimly (dreaming) while a corn-crake (digging in the field-perfume. Dimly) and:

Trains go thundering (under the white Seine cliffs yes?) distantly to Paris and the canalboats and (the Epte is it far away? (for example) that day when we all paddled down from Aveny?) and:

A cock's crowing throws a barbwire entanglement about the moon she thought (always at two o'clock) and the summer-blanketing air heaves in gauzy patterns as (she and the pock-marked trees tossing restlessly) sleeplessly she thought:

This was where he walked. This was where he slept. This was where he drank calvados and played chess. This was where he made the bookshelves for me. This was where he (died?) From distant piers great ocean liners draw out; the bands all playing. And he has gone she thought:

Yet it is in the Seine at Paris nevertheless that all this lies mirrored: but (not for consolation) there is the low booming of the mill-wheel and people (playing an accordeon? . . . la valse brune. Les chevaliers de la lune. . . ?) going crinkling laughing homeward down past toward Monet's. He is in (New York?) she thought:

It is only sometimes these moods she remarked afterward but one second can split into millionths and at night (in the (dreaming) Giverny air) from her pillow the landscape tautens (rubberbandlike) to his feet wherever walking and she lay taut silent for a gesture cuts and (it snapping (one must accustom one's self?) recoiling) where she in this cupped town: and the night:

◈

But I above through the plaited roofs from the hillside I (my eyes like a diver's pointed hands) saw:

My eyes saw:

Saw the white body:

The white body opening woundlike in the darkness:

The white body featherlike drifting:

The white body a compass needle swaying:

The white body a web across the couch:

The couch in the studio:

The studio where I had drunk calvados I had made bookshelves I had slept I had played chess:

I think dreams:

(One must accustom one's self?)

❖

There was a rush of air as she raised her head and her hair circling out across continents

❖

1. He walked into the room porcelain-green from yesterday's twilight and showing his badge the clerk with two eyes like coffee-spoons over a glassy counter—"Send this telegram to Police Headquarters, New York"

❖

2. Thomas K. Merkle and wife walking home on South Water Street Hungerford, N. J. from

the Photoma Palace where they had seen 'Broken Bonds' starring Tom Mix and Bessie Love a Paramount Feature were suddenly startled in the quiet night by a loud roaring buzzing seeming to be approaching rapidly from out the sky directly overhead.

"My God!" cried Mr. Merkle with great presence of mind pulling his wife under a tree whence looking up they presently discerned the gleaming body structure of an enormous aeroplane dashing earthward out of the night at terrific speed.

For a moment Terror tugged at his gullet. Then with a sigh of relief Mr. Merkle (the machine was at this time he afterward testified so close that the features of the aeronaut could be clearly observed peering from behind his wind screen) saw the awesome object zoom suddenly upward clearing by a hair's breadth (so it seemed) the machicolated cornice of the Hungerford Hardware Supply Company Building. It vanished, headed roughly E. S. E.

After a moment spent in regaining their shattered equilibrium as well as in readjusting their garments disarrayed in the first frenzied leap for

safety the good couple proceeded directly homeward and to bed. Mrs. Merkle however (so great
had been the shock of the nocturnal apparition)
for some days after was subject to sudden fainting fits followed by chills in the extremities rack-
ing headaches retching and vomiting of so severe
a character that at one time her life was considered seriously to be in danger.

◇

3. Charles Dograr doubled the corner of Park
Avenue and Fifty-Third Street and glanced back
hastily to see if he were being followed. There
were only a few hours left now. Somehow. . . .
something . . . it was as if things were closing
in. His own footsteps seemed but the echo of
another's passage.

Behind him, the street was vacant. But down
Park Avenue, toward the Grand Central, a man
in a dark suit made his solitary way. Charles Dograr studied that expressionless back like a dog
sniffing a trail. Things were closing in. When
the sun is setting, a man's shadow goes before

him. Was he being paced—not tracked—by the detectives?

But it (this sense, this illusion (if you choose (and as he tried to persuade himself) to call it) that gripped him) was subtler far than that. Rather the variables in his soul's equation were x-ing out at last, and that constant factor which before he had never comprehended he—at the moment of grasping it—was perceiving to diffuse itself in the aura of another's personality; to dissolve itself in the flux of some unseen will stronger than his own as (some dream-personage unremembered. . . . ?) (throbbing black and the white needle-like. . . ?) (a woman . . . no surely. . . ?) (and blue. . . . ?)—if—(blue signs . . . ?) the energy of (blue waters. . . ?) another's purpose were infusing slowly, inexorably into his own.

Charles Dograr (again) thought it was God. (Again) he was wrong.

And now, doggedly, he sets his way in the footsteps of the man in the dark suit ahead.

There are only a few hours left now.

◈

4. A glare of dusted illumination, shuttling over a kaleidoscope of green and blue and yellow, spiraling round a spreading oval pearled with laughing faces and then sprayed waterspoutlike up to the crossed tangle of cordage, the bellying convexities of the Big Tent. Thuds, cries, the taut march of a panther, a deep-throated growl followed by a spring as the Miraclomas, in the center ring, put the big cats through their act.

Mechanically, Adeline Laggick stepped aside in the runway as the Eight Turners herded their twelve white horses out toward the wagons, even now preparing for departure. Their act was over. Hers was yet to come.

The streaking aerial silvered figures, the smell of sawdust calcium jungle-fur greasepaint manure sweaty clothes bran, the glazed hat of the ringmaster, applause, the gilded parade, the deep-set night pallor. . . .

She turned with meditative eyes to the face of Les' Dinkle, a clown, grinning cheerfully at her beneath the grotesque makeup.

"Are you married, Les'? Have you any children?" she asked impulsively, with a naïveté new to her.

The clown's face grew suddenly grave.

"Yes," he replied slowly, "I'm married, Ad'. Married to the gamest little woman this whole world holds. And kids. . . ? Say, I've got seven of 'em, countin' the twins, and take it from me, you can't beat 'em. Here, I'll show you a picture of the youngest. Always carry it with me."

But even as he fumbled in the voluminous folds of his costume, a bell clanged behind him. On the instant, with the instinct of an old 'Trooper,' he stiffened, forgetting all else.

"My 'turn,' Ad,'" he exclaimed. "Show you another time." And he was off, tumbling and stumbling as, with sidesplitting mimicry, he played the part of a policeman in pursuit of an equally amusing burglar.

Adeline watched a moment. A telegram was thrust into her hands. Opening, she read: "Meet me Erie Pa tonight twelve. Am on the trail. Cousin Herbert." She gasped.

The bell clanged. Her crimson cloak dropped from the lovely shoulders, revealing the tracery of gold and gauze that adorned but not concealed her quivering figure. Sidling sidewise, hips swaying, she advanced under the hot glare of a hundred incandescents to do her last 'turn.'

But even as the flageolet and tambourine throbbed in a desert love song—even as the bangles clashed and shivered, shimmering in the rotating movement of her high-swinging breasts —even as the dance grew wilder and the strings of imitation pearls about her hips swished and clattered at the retching looping of her toggling loins and the rosette of pink ribbon sewn just below the small of her back flapped and quivered with the rhythmic revolving of her behind and her whole body was rippling and trembling, the very incarnation of unlicensed desire—even then and through it all, till she stood, spent and panting, listening to the roar of applause at the impassioned finale—the words of that telegram, borrowing the cadence of the dance, were repeating themselves in her mind: "Meet me Erie Meet me Erie Meet me Pa. tonight. Meet me twelve tonight Meet Me."

Once, the tones of the clown, too, came to her

as with unstudied sincerity he had told her of his wife and kiddies. But she had put that aside. Hardly waiting for an encore, she skipped, all flushed and beautiful, to the exit.

Then a glance at her watch. Ten-forty-five. She could just make it.

◈

5. Two men in the turmoil of the noon crowds at Grand Central converging. They brush shoulders. A quick handclasp; unnoticed a scrawled slip of paper is thrust into waiting fingers. Unnoticed? Charles Dograr had been right behind. Without a moment's delay, he followed the larger of the two, a tall heavy-set blonde man wearing a derby hat. Outside, the man leaped into a waiting motor car. Charles stayed long enough to notice that the license plate bore the insignia of the New York Police Department. Then, giving the driver orders to "follow the car ahead" he leaped into a waiting taxicab. Both were swallowed up in the traffic of Forty-Second Street.

◈

6. The ticket-seller in the railway station of a small country town looked out through his grating at the flushed, thickly painted feminine face that moved into line with his, then down at the ten-dollar bill an exquisitely manicured hand had shoved across his counter.

"Yeou be one o' them there circus peepul, ain't ye, Miss?" he queried with half a leer.

"None of your god damned business!" replied the girl. "Give me a ticket to Erie, Pennsylvania."

❖

7. A chance phrase often reveals, in an unguarded moment, more of a man's character than could hours of conscious analysis. The old gentleman known now to us as Picrolas once remarked: "A rose is loveliest in the parabolic moment when, decapitated by your walking stick, it sails for a yard or two through the sunlight and then falls, ruined, in the dust."

This idea, at once so beautiful and so repellent, withal so insouciant, illustrates more than any comment the forces at work in the old gentleman's mind at the moment:

He is seated at his desk (or table) in the window of his room at the lodging house on West Twenty-Third Street. He looks out on the street as if he heard (as indeed he does) some young men practicing the ukelele on the porch below.

Pen and paper lie before him. He is writing a poem, or a letter to Charles Dograr, or an apologia for his career (the facts were never clearly known). Suddenly he bursts into tears. His head falls forward on the desk. Heavy sobs rack his body.

Now his head rises from the couch of his crossed arms. His eye falls on the x-ray machine. A bitter sneer twists his lips, which form the words: "What—has—this—profited—me?"

He rises. He seizes a hammer. With a quick movement he swings it above his head; is about to bring it down on the delicate mechanism. A fit of coughing shakes him. He leans against the table for support till the spasm shall pass.

("Why? . . . Why? . . ." he gasped, like a infant wonderingly. A cold tentacle of phlegm lapped against his palate and a retching convulsion squirmed into his throat. For a moment he struggled literally for breath. "If—I can—last—long enough. Only a—few hours—more!")

Again the weight of hatred tautens his courage. He flings the hammer to a far corner of the room. He strides to the desk; tears up the paper on which he had been writing. For a moment he stares down into the street below. His back is turned to the camera, but his hands are seen to clench with rage. He turns, raises his fist above his head. His lips form the words: "Curse—Charles—Dograr! He—has—spurned—me!"

With extreme care, he begins polishing the glittering accoutrements of the machine.

(Iris out on the machine)

❖

8. A telephone girl at the switchboard. A light flashes. She plugs in.—"Long distance from Erie? Aw ri'. . . . Yeah, this Plice Headquarters. Whosi' for? . . . Huh? . . . The Chief? . . . Aw ri' . . . Waitaminit. You'll get yeh connection." She plugs in the wire for the Chief's Office, twitches the call-bell lever.

XIII—LE KERMES DE L'YEUSE

IN the studio they were·all drinking but (as she
stepped like falling out) on the balcony (behind her the treacherously lighted room a
bomb in the night and) clutching the chill iron
railing she:

(Inside weaving back and forth they laughing
they were all dancing and singing Teddy Pierre
Jim Lily they were all drinking) the stars like
shark's teeth smiled at her. It is cool she felt and
(patting down her breasts her breathing sides to
the trickling flanks) the whiskbroom breeze as
(inextricably intermingled with trees they were
all tight) tumbling (the light striped with
laughter spread fanlike) they:

La viande qui   *here*   well
    put on that   here   *that's*   I like
c'est   Blue Blowers record   *my*   who's got
pas   dance?   *'sais pas*   more punch?   *glass!*

rigolo   open that other   *bonnes d'enfant*
maybe   baby   calvados
baby maybe   don't mean   baby
maybe

she here (if for a while no) no I am not (no
one) not drunk but: her throat fluffed rigidly
against that last glass of (sweetish: and her mind
softening like a tremulously uprearing cone
gelatinous) slightly painful but: it must be balanced:

(I shall not be drunk she thought: Where was
he?) she thought:

(As with (almost) tears) here he died (as she
remembering: Ah! It had been wonderful in the
old days!) remembering: the arm behind her
back his legs (hooked) into hers while (the night
like a shawl about her shoulders and) the writh-
ing filmy night. I said yes. I always (and) looking down:

It fell to earth and bred millions of little white
moths about her eyes (I am not (crying I am
not) drunk. He has gone) but:

It became four stories and kneading (the balcony becoming a window) into a tall brownstone old house: it would be a bedroom: it would be pinkshaded: the girl wears blue: and (carefully) adjusting (her head like the kermès de l'yeuse hardening) and her arms against the cold granite windowsill. She looks down as that other shall do four stories into (where was he? West Twenty-Third Street?) and:

It is West Twenty-Third Street so for a few minutes she offers up hours and hours of watching (before the next dance) a vicarious sacrifice to Love. She produced:

1. Late into the night, Hélène Montmorency remained at her window, staring across the light-lichened expanse of Twenty-Third Street at the House of Mystery opposite.

Sometimes the ripe red lips parted in a sigh. Sometimes a whisper, scarce louder than a sigh, issued from that perfect throat—"He will come soon now"—and, faintlier-flying than her swarming hopes, lost itself on the nigrescent air as she settled again (unconscious of that other who with deft fingers the creamy shoulder modeling, shaping the soft voluted throat across miles and her head dreaming) to the lonely vigil. And still the grim house across the way concealed its secret.

That there was danger she knew. So much she had read in the curl of Fred's predatory lips, in the exultation of his glance as, with scarce a word to her, he had dashed into the room, seized his pistol and hurried out to the street again.

There, from her window she had seen him— strangest sight of all on that strange night!— cross the street and disappear behind the heavy portal of the House of Mystery. And when, at last, he had reappeared, it had been arm in arm with that one—Charles Dograr as we know, his name to her unknown— to whom one night she had thrown sweet kisses and, breathless with passion, had seen him fling the honeyed swarm back from his lips to hers again!

Fred—with the man she loved! A thousand surmises sued her reason for a tardy credence. The man she loved, and the man who loved her, walking arm in arm together! Had Fred forsworn his duty? Had he been won over by bribes —by the cunning persuasion of that old gentleman whom she saw, from time to time behind his window, spiderlike at work among the webbed mechanism of his strange machine? Had he—but no! With all his faults, Fred Coolan prized above aught else the Honor of the Force. And besides, that Captaincy of Detectives—his dream for many years—he had said would be the guerdon of a successful capture. And that he suspected these two across the way of responsibility for the Electric Murders that had terrorized the city, there was no doubt.

Had he trapped them, then? Had he wormed his way cunningly into their confidence, that he might learn their plans and then betray them? If so, only a miracle at this late hour could save the youth she loved from destruction—or worse.

But rather, had they, by superior cunning, misled the detective and tangled his feet in the net of their persuasion? She watched and wondered, waited and watched. Three o'clock boomed from the Metropolitan Tower (or the mill, is it the Epte? pulsing across the fringing perfumed fields? she weaving?) waiting:

"He won't be long . . . now. . . ."

Love, of all the passions flesh is heir to—Love alone could furnish a flame so intense at once and so enduring, to keep those long hours warm with hope, alight with expectancy.

Hélène Montmorency, her body, soiled by contact with a world that is hard and dreary enough for the most fortunate of us, but to none harder, to none drearier than to an orphan foundling cast forth at an early age from the doors of a heartless institution instead of a mother's fond love, penniless, into a brutal world, had grown callous under Life's buffetings.

But deep in the inner core of her weary heart one shrine she had kept pure. And here now, as before an altar, she burned before his image the incense of her adoration.

"Soon . . . now." And shifting slightly in her cramped position as (carefully unfolding the satin fold of her kimono slipping revealing the snow-white softness of that matchless shoulder, the incipient curve of the lifting breasts and like moons in syzygy the crescent curves of thigh and abdomen where scented like pineapple, downy-fragrant like fields cupped beneath the strobile

night and with soft weaving fingers modeling as
(there are people crinkling laughing on the road
"I shall look like a stork here staring white" and
still down) waiting:

Sense ye not, Hélène Montmorency, that silent watching figure—miles, miles away, 'tis true,
in flesh, but near, so near, in dream and thought?
Feel ye not, Hélène Montmorency, those weaving fingers, softly threading thy marble-veined
limbs with life, cushioning thy proud, ripe
breasts within the silken shift and offering all,
in the amorous Night, to the distant lover?

And you, Charles Dograr, danger forgotten,
the chase forsaken, the lust of gold, the heat of
passion stilled at last—what hidden Will now
leads you back down the silent street and makes
you pause a moment, unnoticing, beneath a certain window ere you cross and enter, to join the
erst loved, now hated, companion of your many
crimes?

◇

2. He stands a moment in the silent street. A
bit of paper flutters down before him. Opening,
reading: "*Beware of the blonde man!*" His fea-

tures express surprise. He looks up. All the windows of the house are dark, tenantless. Shaking his head, as one confronted by an insoluble riddle, he crosses the street. Lets himself into Mystery House with latchkey.

◇

3. Within an upper chamber of the House Across The Way, a girl in a blue silk chemise kneels by her bedside. The room is dark. Only a single moonray, stealing through the open window, illuminates the sobbing shoulders, gilds like an aureole the straying, silken hair.

She is praying and, as she prays, scalding tears flow streaming down the shell-pink cheeks. She raises her eyes, her clasped hands to Heaven. Her face, torn by emotion, moves convulsively. Her lips form the words: "Save—him—from—danger."

Fade-out

◇

4. Press-room of metropolitan paper. Men hurrying to and fro with spiked sheets, rolling hogsheads of ink back and forth, etc. Foreman

of press-room stands beside stopped presses, with order for make-up in his hand. Gesticulates angrily, looking at watch. Assistants surround him, deprecatory.

Caption:

> *"Half an Hour Past Deadline Now.*
> *First Time The Paper's Been Held*
> *Up In Years."*

❖

5. City-room of paper. Rows of reporters at typewriters; eye shades; throw sheets of paper hastily into copy baskets. Desk (R.U.E.) City Editor, shirt sleeves, smoking cigar, reading galleys. Looks at watch. Calls star reporter to his side.

Caption:

> *"How About That City Mercantile*
> *Bank Story? If We Hold The Presses*
> *Till Midnight And They Don't*
> *Make The Arrest. . . ."*

❖

6. Reporter smiles. Hands sheets of typed paper to Editor.

Caption:

> *"Here's The Lead For The Story.*
> *The Chief Of Police Told Me They*
> *Have The Gang Under Their Thumb*
> *And They'll Pinch Them All When*
> *They Try To Rob The Bank. It's*
> *A Sure Thing."*

❖

7. Editor looks doubtful. Shakes Head. Takes sheets from reporter; scans them; begins to smile approvingly.

❖

8. *Close-up flash of story;*

X-RAY MURDERER CAUGHT AT LAST
Scientific Criminal and Accomplice
Arrested on Threshold
of Big Hold-Up

One Hundred Shots Fired On Crowded
Thoroughfare. Police Make
Long-Awaited Arrest As
Thousands Stare.

At an hour a little past midnight, as he stood surrounded by eighteen victims

on the threshold of his greatest *coup,*
René Fonstant, alias Benjamin Constantin, Thorndyke Smithers, Edouard
Percy, James Butler, Arthur Moss, etc.,
etc., met justice at last.

Two police cars swung around a corner loaded with policemen, as he was
transferring nineteen millions in specie
from a looted armored car into a waiting motor car before the City Mercantile Bank, and after a furious pistol
battle in which nine policemen and two
bystanders were wounded, succeeded in
putting under arrest the most dangerous and brutal murderer in the history
of crime.

With him was his young accomplice,
alias Charles Dograr. Both stand
charged with the astounding total of
sixty-seven murders, all committed—
by means of some as yet unknown
mechanism permitting electrocution by
radio—within the short space of two
months. They pleaded 'Not Guilty,'

and it is said that eminent legal aid will be called in to their assistance in what promises to be one of the most sensational trials of the century. Fonstant himself, as he was. . . .

❖

9. Editor looks up from copy, smiling.

Caption:

"It's A Good Story. We'll Wait For It. Better Run Down To The Bank And Be On The Spot When They Pull It Off."

❖

10. Steps of rooming house on West Twenty-Third Street. A fuzzy little man ascends to door, rings bell. Landlady opens. They talk.

Caption:

"Can I Get A Room Here, Ma'am?" Landlady opens door wider. He goes in, after hasty glance, as of one hunted, around and up and down street. It is Rupert Pragman.

❖

11. Solemnly (circling the hills and bluegray fields behind) Binghampton; Utica; Syracuse;

Troy a man ploughing and (cleaving (a white road where the red and green buckboard spick-and-span is pawing) the horizon) and: *click*-toc-toc-*click*-toc-toc-*click*-toc-toc-*click*

From here and there scattering the lights went on: with a shattering roar of wheels couplers grinding whirling axles following: between the dead blank walls of a factory Eastman's Soap. It was Amsterdam and on:

"When do we reach New York?"

"Well, boss, we was thutty minutes late outa Erie but we made up fifteen minutes already. Ah raickon we'll pull in awn time at tenfawty. Yessuh."

Herbert Trask, seated in the railway carriage, glances impatiently at his watch. Half past nine.

❖

12. Office of Chief of Police. Large, handsome man with irongray mustache. In uniform, seated at mahogany desk. Picks up telephone and twiddles hook. Then talks into receiver.

❖

13. Precinct police station. Police lieutenant at desk, writing in blotter. Several policemen tunics unbuttoned lounge in chairs. (It is a heavy-angled room as if it suspended tons of masonry and in an egg-yellow illumination; policemen always look as if they had just finished stew and dumplings for dinner and these in the scene their faces belch at the vacant walls) Lieutenant answers phone. Speaks, nodding deferentially—Yes, yes, yes. Snaps receiver back on hook, summons policeman.

Caption:

"Stand By For A Riot Call. Chief Says They're Going to Pinch Them Radio Murderers Tonight!

❖

14. There was a knock on the door. Hastily concealing his test-tubes in a drawer and (throwing a cloth shrouding the outlines of the x-ray machine—"Come in," the old gentleman called and) the door opening.

A smallish man his face emerging from a light

fuzzy gray suit like a moth from its cocoon was standing there. He was casting quick furtive glances at the apparatus of the room.

"Well?" and a suspicion worcestershire-sauce-like the old gentleman at his heart as—"Is. . . . is this the . . . ah . . . Seaside Employment . . . Agency?" The man's voice ran down the words like a timorous spider down its thread.

"No!" barked the old gentleman. "I'm busy."

The little man hesitated.

"I'm busy. Get out!"

But for a long time afterward. . . .

◈

15. "This is the last time," he had said. He had gone away and left her. Running with brilliant rapidity through her mind in the short space between the Manager's Office and her dressing room, Adeline Laggick had lived over again the events of that afternoon on the Palisades, spent in the arms of the man she now knew to be her uncle's murderer.

Her flesh crawled as she thought of it . . . his kisses . . . faugh! (She wipes her lips at the re-

membrances, expressing disgust) . . . the nest-
ling tug of his hip into hers . . . this man, this
Dograr, as Herbert had said he called himself—
was a coward, a cur, and yet . . . was it true,
what the doctor had said—that she would bear a
child to this monster? . . . Would she pay the
price of the shameful thing she had done on that
moon-darkened evening? . . . Oh! . . . And
children. . . .Les' Dinkle . . . what was it he
had said? . . .

So, her face gray and weary beneath the greasepaint . . . and here Dinkle himself, waiting
sheepishly before the door of her dressing-room.
. . . Good old Les' . . . Her heart warmed at
his honest eyes. . .

"I was waitin' to show you that snap o' my
youngest kid, Ad," he brought out awkwardly.
And added, still more sheepishly. "Say, Ad! I
was figurin' out a darn' good number you an'
me could do together—supposin' . . ." he hesitated painfully. . . . "Supposing you an' me
was to . . . you know . . . get married an
. . . go into vaudeville together. . . ." He
looked beseechingly up at her.

"But you're already married, aren't you, Les'?" she queried, wondering.

"Aw, sure . . . but my wife's a Mormon. We was married out in Salt Lake."

A sudden revulsion seized her. Men were all alike. And this Dograr. . . . Once she had thought. . . . But she could not bring herself to hurt this honest heart.

"We could try it out here . . . you know . . . work it up with the circus before we jumped."

"It's too late for that, Les'," she answered sadly. He stared in amazement. "I got the can five minutes ago."

"You! Fired! Why, but listen. . . ." he was stuttering, sobbing, in his mingled wrath and amazement. "Listen, Ad', you got your contrac'."

"Evans says it's cancelled. You see, I jumped the show last night, to—to meet my cousin in Erie, Pa."

"Aw, but say, Ad'. . . ."

It wrenched her heart. But the mission now before her . . . she must purge herself of all the softer passions . . . she must forge her mind, her body to the instrument of Hate. For a moment sorrow blinded her eyes and she stared with infinite compassion at the honest face before her. Then—

"It's too late, Les'. I'll remember you. Good-by. Good-by!" A wrenching handclasp, tearing her soul—and his. She was gone!

XIV—MIDNIGHT

THE City Mercantile Bank on Warren Street is one whose name figures small indeed in the financial activities of a city whose bank clearances often exceed a billion dollars daily.

Founded in 1802, it still remains in the modest, though solidly-constructed building of brick and brown-stone, while its more prosperous brothers rear skyscraper temples and scatter branch agencies, glittering with brass and glass, throughout the city.

In the City Mercantile the accretion of 127 years has produced only a slightlier musty tang in the unhurried atmosphere, a deeper polish on the worn and furrowed mahogany of the counter fittings and (seemingly) a more rheumatic curve in the bent backs of the tellers at their windows and of the clerks in the counting room. Everyone seems old there.

But though its whole equipment be fifty years out of date; though its personnel abound in quinqua- (even septua-) genarians; though it make no attractive offers to gain new depositors, yet there still flows a goodly volume of money through the worn gratings of its teller's windows.

For, at its founding, James R. Stacker, its first president, was a power in the then financial world of New York. Came readily to him as clients the then most influential business houses of the day. And though many of these have fallen in the rising tide of competition, there are many as well who have thrived and prospered in the century's passage.

And of these, all—through regard for the unflinching honesty of an unbroken line of Stackers at its head; through perhaps a touch of sentiment at thought of the old bank's history— have continued as clients of the City Mercantile.

It will be seen, then, that the City Mercantile Bank occupies a position unique in the financial world. Its list of clients is small, but immensely wealthy. Its transactions, though infrequent, are always for immense sums. Its vaults, though pitifully antiquated, are alternately empty, or bursting with huge gold deposits.

Couple this with an ingrained obstinacy among its personnel, from President Stacker down to the aged doorman, against new methods—credit them with an utterly unjustified conviction that the crime problem of the modern city is as simple as it was in the year 1805, and it will readily be understood that the 'cannon' (vice: 'stick-up man'—'highwayman') spoke truth when he said "I could take a brass band along and lift the works!"

❖

1. "I don't see why they don't come along and get this over with. All these guns and battleship armor-plate! Newfangled notions! Why, in my day. . . ." The hour was eleven-thirty. The speaker was James Miller, for forty-two years chief teller of the bank.

"Now, Mr. Miller," Henry Gray, the night watchman interrupts. Old in the service as the other, he permits himself many minor liberties. "Don't you go and get yourself all het up about it. You know they ain't due here 'till twelve, an' it's only ha'past eleven now. And listen here," he added as an afterthought, "You jus' go inside an' set down where it's warm 'f you don't want to get your rheumatiz' back again! Standin' outside in this night air!"

"You shut up, Henry Gray! I'm not worrying about my rheumatism when I got nineteen millions in gold pieces to get off my hands." Nevertheless he turns back to the interior where a portable oil stove has been lighted in the lobby of the bank, to warm the watchers. Around its cheery glow five men are grouped—four special policemen and Mr. Blodgett, the assistant teller. The youngest of the group, he is 47 years old, has served in the World War and has been twice decorated for bravery under fire. We shall hear more of him later. The others, stretching their gnarled old hands out to the flames, the old jaws working rhythmically over the individual 'chaw' of tobacco, look more like a chatty group of codgers gathered beside some country stove, than the guardians of a treasure surpassing the wildest dreams of avarice.

Only the rifles, stacked in the corner against

the counter, and the cavernous, shadowy interior lend a sinister touch to the scene.

"What time is it, Blodgett?" asks Miller. "I swan, boys, I feel oneasy tonight, I do. Like as if something untoward was about to happen."

◈

2. Charles Dograr rises from the chair-arm lunch and fending aside the reverberating brilliance of the indigestible tile walls he makes his way to the (it is cool dark on the slippery pavement and) the long loop of Lexington Avenue. A motor car has drawn to the curb. He steps on the running board, climbs in as with gathering speed it turns down Twenty-Second Street:

◈

3. An instant of blackness. The side curtains are down. The glow of a cigarette against a blued jaw:

Caption:

"*Where Is The Blonde Man?*"

Nobody seems to answer and the man negligently puffing a lungful of smoke and there is a kind of murderous waiting amusement in his attitude.

Caption:

"*Aw, He Said He'd Meet Us Downtown.*"

◈

4. But one would swear the air is shaking are they laughing? The traffic lights on the Avenue switch to red. Smoothly the car swerves into a side street. "What time is it?"—"Twenty minutes to."

◈

5. With a sweep and a (sidewise) bumping. To the eye of its bluecoated occupant the wings strumming steady and: the world oscillates and especially (the Times Square Building like a topheavy pendulum swinging between black roofs) the electric signs: the Y of rushing streetway. Swiftly the airplane rises: circles: speeds south.

◈

6. A flash to the old gentleman in the still room: the light like butter smeared across the

angled jaw. All passion chills against the eyes
(like icicles) etching the machine against the
yellow walls. His hands softly moving adjusting.
Slowly the swivelled barrel swings. It hums. The
ray moves out.

He smiles (but his smile shattered by a cough
and) a bitter horror. His gaze steadies trium-
phant. Again to the oculascope.

Caption:

> *With Infinite Care He Centers The
> Mechanism On His Intended Victims.*

7. A shuttling sweep of windows blinking as
(the spurt of people hurrying (among them
Herbert and Adeline) and) EXPRESS SOUTH
FERRY. They are jammed aboard and (gleaming
down the black nozzle (shimmering with darkness) of the tunnel) where the red lights dis-
appearing.

"Are we in time?" she had cried. For a moment
his strong arm had held her; his eye gazed into
hers. "Oh! Herbert! Avenge me! His death alone
can purge my body of its shame! Avenge me,

and I am yours—all yours!" And leaping together.

◆

8. Fred rushes in on Hélène. She, watching, has only time to hear his half-uttered cry of exultation before: his feet tumbling downstairs in the quiet. One glance to the street. She leaps to her feet.

Caption:

"*I Must Save Him!*"

And hastily fastening a dress about her chilled form, a hat pushed over her tousled silky hair. She follows. Whither?

◆

9. "Here comes the armored car, Mr. Miller!" "Wha-what? Where?" He had been dozing. "Right outside now. They're unloading."

◆

10. The man in the airplane saw it all. Revolving slowly and the street like a magnetic needle pointing to an inconstant north as it swung, he saw far down (and the buildings like inverted cones mutually intersecting) at:

The shiny-hard beetle-backed armor of the truck at the curb. It was exactly midnight. He saw the guards step out of the slotted doors. They spaced the vacant sidewalk. From the bank (seen above, circling) the bustling little figures with peeping feet and floating shoulders. Four special policemen a man in a gray uniform a man in brown a man in black in diminutive eddies around where:

A door has swung open. The sacks are dumping out. The man in the airplane sees it all and hastily dot-dot-dashing the news to Headquarters where a man with an irongray mustache:

❖

11. Hélène slipping from doorway to doorway follows Fred down the street. He pauses at the corner. She, shrinking into a store entrance sees a gray car swoop to the curb. A moment's colloquy. Fred leaps in. Hastily she leaps into a waiting taxi. "Follow the car ahead!"

❖

12. And now in his cupola of silence the old gentleman he makes the last adjustment and chuckling:

Caption:

"*Charles Shall Die—Last Of All!*"

His treacherous mirth. His eye settles to the oculascope. Like a snake to strike the whole coiled mechanism. His hand closes on the insulated lever. Down!

Caption:

"*One!*"

And (but before he again) he moves a switch and the Dead Plane cupping dimming over his (one sees moving spidery within the Plane) his face white opaque as:

❖

13. No one had seen that the driver of the armored truck but: and his hands as if taking away. A kind of liquid blueness his face. Unobserved, a powerful motor car quietly stealing had crept abreast the truck on the opposite side of

the street. Charles Dograr leans out. Across the way and a guard whirling; his hand drops to the holster but: like a kick in the forehead and: as if a box of matches igniting all at once his face. Charles laughed aloud. All turned:

◈

14. To explain why, at this particular moment, Mr. Thomas K. Merkle should have decided to walk down Warren Street we must recall to the reader's mind the fainting, choking, vomiting fits to which his wife had been subject, and which had been induced, in all probability, by the strange airplane which had swooped down over them the previous night in Hungerford, N. J., and vanished. In further justification of what may seem at first an unpermissible coincidence, we may state that inventory-taking at the plumbers'-fittings store in which Mr. Merkle worked had necessitated late hours among its clerks—and that Mr. Merkle had promised, on returning homeward, to stop at an all-night drugstore on Warren Street to get a prescription filled, before taking the ferry.

He saw ahead of him, fulcruming the tilted, deserted street, the blue-painted racer, the big black truck standing side by side. He noticed, wondering, the moving group of figures, the opened bank doors. And, darting with a spurt of terror through his bewilderment, with a glance overhead he made out the dim-shining wing-structure, heard the muffled roar of the airplane circling overhead.

"What's up, I wonder?" Mr. Merkle asked himself. The question was never answered. As he advanced, he saw a man fall; sprawl grotesquely on the sidewalk. It was a man in a black suit. Another reached; leaned; crumpled. A man with a brown belt over a blue uniform skipped toward the shelter of the truck, tugging at his belt; then as if he had suddenly gone lame and pitched into the gutter. There was also a man in gray lying on the bank steps. Another. Another.

Dimly, Merkle realized that he was present at a holocaust. But he saw no firing, heard no shots. Across the street, leaning out of the racing car, a young man was watching, smiling.

Merkle suddenly wanted to run, to shout, to

hide, to hit the young man's smiling lips. At the same moment, paralyzing all motion except his slow onward stepping came the flash: "It's the Electric Murderers!" and "Mary's tonic! I must get out of this!"

A man came out of the bank door as if he had been thrown out; his body slammed down in an ungainly heap at the foot of the steps. Two young men had climbed out of the racing car, were leisurely loading heavily-padlocked sacks from the truck into the tonneau of their car. The smiling young man was lighting a cigarette.

Merkle realized he had not yet been noticed. A frenzy of fury began to mount in his heart. Like a man pointing a gun, deliberately, he aimed his wrath at the young man. The airplane's roar overhead was diminishing. No one was in sight. Midway of the street the two gunmen and the sack they were carrying dropped lumping together.

At this, the young man standing still, now alone, beside his car, became oddly audible. Merkle comprehended that it was laughter. His rage soared to his arms like wings. From behind

the armored car he plunged full on the defence-
less Charles Dograr.

Charles had not even time to raise his arms.
He saw the contorted face, the flailing arms flung
suddenly at him out of blackness—saw the apparition sweep at him, full of vengeful life—saw
the head jam sidewise in mid-career—and was
nearly overturned as the lifeless body slumped
heavily against him, tottered, and fell slowly at
his feet. There was a blue mark on the forehead!

For a moment, Charles was too confused to
reason. "Eighteen! Eighteen!" he murmured
slowly. "But then this man. . . . Why is the old
gentleman aiming this way? . . . If this guy
hadn't come in between . . . pushed me back.
. . . Why, he's already got his. . . . Why . . .
why . . . the old murderer must—have—been
—aiming—at—me!" The conclusion was obvious.

"At me!"

And then, as with the snap of a switch, he was
galvanized into sudden furious energy. If the old
gentleman was (as indeed he had been) aiming
the x-ray gun at Charles, there was no time to be

lost. He leaped to the driver's seat, threw in the gear. The car swung grinding round the corner and away.

A moment later, the gray police car hurled into the deserted street.

Fred, standing braced against the windshield, gave a hasty glance around; cursed.

"They got away!" he cried. The car swooped to the corner. Far, far up Broadway, he saw the speeding fugitive. "There he goes! Give her the gas, Jim!"

◈

15. "Nineteen!" With a horrible chuckle, the old gentleman leans back from the mechanism as: and with like thunder cries: as—the door hammering. He reaches for the Dead Plane lever. There is not time! A tall stranger a painted flashing girl through the split panels. An X of tugging hands over the lever. Slowly, the old gentleman's feebler fingers give way.

"Where has he gone?"

"Who?"

The girl sweeps between, her face afire with hate. "You know who! Dograr! Your pal!"

The man draws her away. "Wait, Adeline. He'll tell." His eye grows menacing. "He'll tell, or. . . ."

The old gentleman laughed. "Tell?" he cackled. "Why shouldn't I tell?" For a moment his old voice broke, sobbed. "Dograr—is—dead!"

Adeline burst into a wild laugh. "I wish I thought so!" she cried, and to the tall man: "Come on, Herbert, don't let him get away with that."

But Herbert had been watching intently. "I think he believes it, Ad," he said. "I think he thinks he killed him. . . ."

The old man's voice cut in, rising to a thin shriek. "Never mind who killed him. He's dead. . . ."

Herbert's fist came down. "Listen, old man. Charles Dograr is driving like mad up Avenue B at this present moment. I know what happened. You aimed your infernal machine to blast the brain of your partner, but at the instant you closed the switch, a man stepped between. You killed Thomas K. Merkle, of Hungerford. N. J.! Charles Dograr is alive!"

"Charles Dograr is alive!"

"Charles Dograr is alive!"

Again the girl, a fury of revenge. "And we want to know where he's gone to. We want to know! You'll tell us, by God! or . . . or. . . ."

The old gentleman had been regarding her half-smiling. "Why," he asked, "why do you want to know where he is?"

Perhaps she sensed the common feeling between them. Abruptly, she ceased her threats.

"Because I hate him," she replied. "He was a beast—yes! worse than a beast to me! I have sworn to kill him!"

"I hate him too," replied the old gentleman simply, wearily. "You will find him at my country house—Greenwood Manor, Bayslip Road, Long Island."

"Straight?"

"I swear—it!" A slight cough had shaken the feeble voice.

"Come on Herbert!" She turned with a whirl of draperies toward the door.

"Wait!" They paused. The old man, his face clenched over his agony, seemed to speak. A fit of coughing plugged his throat a moment. Then—

"Go by—the Queens—Bridge. Take—the— Flushing cutoff. You'll catch—him. Kill. . . ."

He waved a hand wearily at them. They were gone, like prestidigitation. He turned, half falling, slumped over the light-box of the machine. Here it was as if his arms and hands exploded. A hammer, the uprooted switch, and his nails clawing at the wires of the antennæ. He struck; pounded, hammered; here, there; brandishing.

(The machine lies in ruins. The old gentleman, pale, staggers; flops inert across the shattered mechanism. A trickle of red flows wormlike from a corner of his mouth, drips silently on the x-ray barrel. Stillness).

◈

16. The man in the airplane saw it all—saw the two cars speeding up the broad reaches of Avenue B, the gray car now gaining, now falling slowly back again as the man crouched low at the wheel of the leading car, the wind like milk slashing past the windshield, he pulls open the

throttle another notch. He saw the taxi, floundering in the wake of all, saw the girl (Hélène) leaning frantically from the door, crying: "Follow! follow! Ten—twenty dollars if you follow them!"

They roar to the Bridge, sweeping up the broad approaches. He glides, circling over the high stone towers as they shuttle through the network of struts and girders and emerge roaring down toward Jackson Avenue and the straightaway out the Island. There, as on a map, they lie below him. He sees the spurt of flame as the man (Fred leaned out, braced against the windshield.—"I'll get the bastard!"—Aimed. Fired. Missed. The car sped on. Fred reloaded. "Step on it! Damn it! Step on it!")

And behind them both, the crawling taxi still hung on. He sees, too, looping swiftly across fields to the Flushing Cut-Off, the fourth car, a man at the wheel, a girl by his side—sees it leap across the chord of the arc the three other cars are following.

He sees the taxi stop, the girl climb out. ("Dis car won't go no foider, miss."—Frantic, she thrusts a roll of bills into the driver's hands. She takes to the fields, running madly blindly to her lover's aid. Rain is beginning to fall. In the darkness heavy like a weight on her shoulders, and she stumbles, falls, staggers to her feet again cut, bruised; she runs on. The wind whips her skirt against her legs; her jacket, her blouse sodden with rain clings chokingly about her. With frenzied haste—"Will I be in time?"—she tears them from her, flings aside the trammeling garments. Clad only in her blue silk chemise, braving cold and sleet and darkness, sobbing panting crying, Hélène Montmorency races toward the man she loves!)

He sees the red car, slipping down the side roads converging, gaining now, and the gray car. Will the flying leader reach his goal in time?

❖

17. He lay where he had fallen. That yellow room the flat paneling of light dropping to the silent figure and his heart (or is it the tapping stick McDowell?) tap-tapping faintlier as: the old gentleman's eyes like glued paper curling

opening. In the doorway is that a human figure? Pragman turns his wiry nose about the door-jamb. He steals into the room. He prowls nervously to the old gentleman. ("Now this is a funny mess. What are these prongs for, I wonder? I always had a leaning for machinery. . . . And here's a little button, too. . . .")

He pressed the button. With a dull roar the building swaying, swept up in a spraying fan of light and Pragman: the old gentleman and: as the explosion shattered: McDowell tap-tapping smiling and: it settled in a crumpled steaming dusty pile of rock and masonry.

❖

18. In a silent room at Headquarters. The Chief stops pacing a moment, pausing beside the desk of the radio operator, the instrument ticking.

"What's the latest, Ed?"

"Dograr making out for the center of the Island. Coolan gaining fast. A red car cutting in on Dograr. Toss-up whether Dograr or the red car gets in first."—A fresh outburst of ticking activity from the instrument.—"Here's news, Chief!" cries the operator excitedly. "The old guy on Twenty-Third Street just blew the house up! Total ruin!"

Expressionless, sombre, the deep eyes of the Chief stare out toward where three fast cars are racing for the stakes of Life or Death!

XV—BESIEGED!—DELIVERED!

H<small>E</small> was running and before the (dim marble staircase like a dissected laugh) hound-like leaping the long corridor had faded into inkily black (and below knock-knock they are) hammering like the throbbing in his brain. His flash-light at last scalloping huge draping walls as doors as (and below if the door they are hammering if it holds firm?) pleating the beam of his light with shadow at last the stairs. The stairs to the tower.—"If I can reach the tower!"

Downstairs the heavy door with a crash of paneling. Like a cat his body crouching in the darkness his feet pivoted for flight he hears the searchers' voices.—"God! I near broke my get your guns ready boys went up this we got him close you look in that Harry no. Up this. Now!" And outside in the silence a sandpaper grate of gravel on the drive a skirl of brakes as wheels spin to a stop. More were arriving! Moments would swing the issue now!

Bolting the tower door and in the feathery darkness he felt step by step mounting as his head through cobwebs. There was a stir of bat-wings in the deep-recessed walls. Something brushed heavily against his face. Behind below he heard their feet pounding as they searched the rooms. Nearer. His head came sharp against the flat wood. But he was beyond pain now. With a frenzied shove, the trap door swung upward and like a silver screen the sky. He was on the tower roof at last. And there:

Or (was it the breeze?) some dark woman dis-tantly moving as her hair inwinding, her per-fumed hair fine-netted enfolding and he:

Across continents some woman (the sky? or whose? those blue ingurgitating eyes?) voice-lessly calling some woman beside blue waters un-dreamed-of melancholy-moving and or that low blue laugh the Seine?

As if the silver mail of her remembrance (the moonlight?) encrusting him. He felt the air warm like the pressure of her (he was asking?)

breasts. Her breasts soft and warm and pointed and he felt (it was all about him) and as if (those enwinding hairs had they threaded deep in the veins of his body?) with a toss of her head he was swaying but across continents:

❖

The man in the airplane (his hand gripping hard on the lever that would release the bomb) he saw it all. He saw the tower top a gleaming disk a reflecting moon among the slope-shadowed angles of the gables. He saw (a dark effigy on the silent tower) the waiting figure of the man they hunted. As he circled and rose again, he saw the dozens of patrolling men, their figures black against the moondusted lawn, saw occasionally the light flash along the barrels of the guns they carried.

To the rear of the house, the red car had nosed deep in the tree-shadows. There a man and a woman, both with pistols ready, sat silent intense waiting their eyes fixed on the vacant windows of the building thenceforth to be known throughout the countryside as the "House Of Dograr's Doom"!

He circled again, and Charles saw the wing surfaces gleam a moment, heeling into the turn, saw the machine drift downwind black like a bat against the moon, saw it swing round again heading stiffly up again to pass (and lower now) over his head.

Charles watched the thrumming monster, his throat choking. Then—a spit of flame from the hedgeshadow—a whip-snap crackle—the singing hiss of a bullet. It flattened against the wall below him. A woman's voice rose clear, exultant:

"Did I get him, Herbert? Did you see?"

A heavy bitterness swung like a pendulum in his stomach. He could not repress a cry:

"Adeline! Adeline!"

Another shot was the reply. And—"Stick your head up, you carrion! I'll give you Adeline!"

That voice . . . and she . . . he had thought.

Things accelerated. They were firing now on all sides. The air was full of bullets. His ear was vibrating with their hissing passage, the flack of impact. He could duck them, yes. But how duck that roaring approaching enemy from above, driving slowly back and forth in ever-tightening spirals overhead? How evade the bombs he knew it carried? And how elude (they were tearing the panels of the tower door below, he heard them hammering) those searchers in the house below, converging toward his hiding place?

Charles Dograr, even as he watched, knew there was no escape. He had but to wait . . . as bravely as he might . . . for annihilation. One thing the fighting Dograr blood assured him: he would never be taken alive!

"I shall die like a man!" he cried, with a clear eye for his Fate. "Say that I died game, boys!" he called down to the policemen massed below. A faint sound of cheering came up to him. But:

"You'll die like the dog you are!" he heard the voice of Adeline crying with vengeful hate. He saw her white hand raised, saw the pistol levelled.

"Shoot, girl!" he cried, stepping forward to the parapet. "Shoot! In the name of the child I gave you! My life for his!" And fearless, his hair atoss with the gentle breeze, his shirt thrown open across his breast he stood there, waiting, for the blow that would lay him low.

Even Adeline, heart-sore with hate as she was, must pause at sight of such magnificent courage as was his. And that moment cost her dear. Even as, at last, the gun in the girl's fair hand spat forth its leaden messenger of death, a crash, a rush of footsteps on the tower behind him made Charles Dograr turn. What new danger was this? Adeline's bullet, forgotten, sped harmlessly over his head. From the mouth of the tower stairway, all blue and pink and beautiful, burst sobbing panting in the open moonlight to fling herself wildly into his arms—Hélène Montmorency, come to cover his lip's last life with kisses, to shield with the warmth of her fair body that of her lover—Hélène Montmorency beautiful and unashamed in the curving redundancy of her body's loveliness beneath the unconcealing silk chemise!

"Girl! Girl!" (as he and with a voice like a phonograph but yielding to those distant weaving fingers he)—"What madness brings you here?"

"Charles! My love! My life! My soul! I could not stay without you. If it be not fated that we live and love together, then grant me this, my last request, that we die—yes, die! here, together!"

She fainted. Still holding her throbbing form pressed close to his as he covered her lips with kisses and raising his eyes to Heaven and but:

(It was as if his eyes diamonds and from a thousand facets his vision gleaming on a world split in as many subtly-varying aspects; example: he perceived for the first time that of this touching scene of which he was the protagonist the background. (viz., the ivy-mantled tower the stone-buttressed walls the hoary trees the lawn velvety to the tread) could be all dismantled at a moment's notice and as when (the showman politely bowing) the curtain rolling up on its mandrel disclosing the:)

And as even Fred too, then, the burly blonde man. His face black with passion. His eyes like coals with rage. He leaped heavily up the stairs and to and thrusting between them:

"You hound! I've caught you at last! Stand

back, Hélène! It's he and I alone now! To the death!"

And but Charles with a vague deprecatory gesture (to be sure (he wonderingly) this girl in my arms now her half-opened lips the lidded eyes back-falling head the swaying back against my sustaining arm all firm, caressing to the touch and her hips (Again that sad gray woman beside blue waters phantom-moving he saw and the deepswimming eyes the weaving viviparous fingers) distant, unremembered he; yet yes! he almost saw her yes clear and threading this fair lovely figure sobbing against my breast as) with a brusk movement (it was as when a swimmer from deep water rising his head through the shell of dreaming darkness and his eyes glazed with light) for a moment bursting but:

The effect upon Charles was narcotic in the extreme. Or perhaps better than by the metaphor of the light-struck swimmer, we can describe his sensations in that curious moment by asking the reader if he (or she) have ever (seated through the indolent afternoon by some smooth-flowing river's side) seen suddenly a fish (fringe-

jawed barbel, slim-backed trout—it matters not)
leap from the current, arch gleaming, and disappear again? It was a spurt of foaming water—
a silver twisting flash against the brush-covered
bank—and, almost before the eye can have
caught the picture, a plashing plunge—a thrust
of the sturdy tail—and it has gone beyond pursuit, skimming the reedy river-bottom, and only
the ripples repercussively lapping the bank beneath our feet remain to attest its passage.

Figure then, that the fish is Charles as we
the watchers; consider that the arching moment
through what to us was sunlight is, to him, blackness; remember that—as to us, plunging, the
water from which he starts—so to him the air
we breathe, too long inhaled, spells suffocation
and death; lastly, note that the spreading after-
ripples which to us, rather than any actual vision
of the leap, serve as basis by which we reconstruct
in our mind's eye the finny apparition, remain
to him only a swift-dimming, swift-narrowing
cone of agitation, pointing deeper but fainter
after him as he swims rapidly farther, deeper in

(to the fish) the stream, or (to Charles Dograr) his dream.

But for Charles Dograr (as for the fish) that swerving flash through the uninhabitable land of remembrance had sufficed. Had sufficed to cool (as the fish its sides) his fevered imagining—had drained the heat of plot and counterplot from out his struggling soul. Though in the flashing moment he had been as one, blinded by too much light, it had yet served to bring before him plain that Other Face—that gray, distant, dreaming woman. Like the lightning flash, its glare had been destructive, breaking the thread of her (to him unremembered) dream, freeing him forever from the almost corporeal imaginings that surrounded him and even as she (far-distant, dreaming) turned the last sheet and closed the book he was walking down Fifth Avenue, smoking a cigar.

END

EPILOGUE

A ND he. . . .
But and she:
Unaccountably, it was as she so often afterward used to tell, but then everything connected with the whole affair a conflict of unprobable impulses, she said: I only write adventure stories I don't want to live them, she said: give me the great open spaces of a Paris street, she said: let my eyes roam over the enormous vistas of the wallpaper in my room on the (and she always remembering: she walking the) rue Lacepède the rue (feeling smotheringly the smooth slipping of silk along the cool flesh of her thighs) Gracieuse the. . . .

It had been just a year. He was undoubtedly and yet he had said:

He had said. . . .

He had (Gentle Reader, we have seen her walking those old streets that fringe the Panthéon; we have seen her moody at the Seine-side, and sleepless in the Giverny air. Always her thoughts had been of him. And now) as:

(Yellowly the heat drip-drip-dripping from the funneling roofs) she held the sky over her head like an umbrella: he (had Oh! all that he) had said. But it had been just as she had supposed. New York too why hadn't she gone? But he had. . . .

It had been a year. She saw lait à volonté in a window and it closed her eyes with sudden tears: and down the rue du Puits-de-l'Ermite and turning. . . .

Glimpsingly she remembered she had (like the kermès de l'Yeuse) imagined a granite window-sill on Twenty-Third: but had it had he: ah! were all men as. . . .

Sorrow corkscrewing she walking: she was re-membering. . . .

◈

To the concierge with a fidgeting welcome:

"Bon jour Celestine."

"Bon jour Madame! And Madame returns so soon from the country?"

"Yes. I was bored." And, automatically: "No news, Celestine?"

And the other ducking in among the little room frying with sauté de veau she reappears with letters.

"Here are many letters for Madame."

She listlessly; but the other's barberish face beaming roguishly: "There is one letter from America. If it is from Monsieur Dograr?"

She could hardly contain herself. He had deserted her and: but he had said (a year) and hastily tearing open the envelop (all thought of concealing her perturbation thrown to the winds as the benevolent smiling the concierge) and all eyes as (ruffling to the signature):

"Yes! Yes! Celestine! It is from Monsieur Dograr after all!"

And then with trembling fingers the (maidenly) and she felt hot flushes mounting to her cheeks as (in his curious writing) here and there: ". . . have been thinking of . . . so much has . . . often wonder if after all I . . . curious sensation the other day. . . . I was walking . . . like a dream . . . overpowering. . . ."

And as the words ran together before the glad tears unnoticed streaming and the soft-hearted concierge. She found herself sobbing on the black alpaca shoulder.

"Oh! Celestine! Was ever happier woman than I? He—he—is coming back!"

Let us leave them thus.

NEW CAPRICORN BOOKS

15. *Anton Chekhov,* ST. PETER'S DAY AND OTHER TALES. For the first time in English, here is a hilarious collection of early Chekhov stories and sketches. Resembling Dickens, Gogol and the Keystone Kops in their comic method, these stories will undoubtedly consolidate Chekhov's growing reputation as a major comic writer. Translated by Frances H. Jones. *A Putnam Capricorn Original.* 224 pp. $1.25 (Hardcover, $2.50).

16. *Thomas Nashe,* THE UNFORTUNATE TRAVELLER, OR JACK WILTON. Edited, with an Introduction, by John Berryman. Illustrated by Michael Ayrton. "The first novel in English" is the claim that has been made for this wonderful book. Published in 1594, it displays Nashe's madly inventive prose style, which has been compared to the style of Joyce's FINNEGANS WAKE, and Nashe's uncanny ability to create marvellously alive personalities. Of the first importance in the history of the novel. *A Putnam Capricorn Original.* 128 pp. $1.15 (Hardcover $2.50).

17. *Simone Weil,* WAITING FOR GOD. With an Introduction by Leslie Fiedler. T. S. Eliot said of it, "This book, by the late Simone Weil, is almost too important to be included in one's list of preferred reading for one year only." Andre Gide said, "It is clear that Mlle. Weil is the most truly spiritual writer of this century." 240 pp. $1.25.

18. *Robert M. Coates,* THE EATER OF DARKNESS, by the author of THE HOUR BEFORE WESTERLY. It is difficult to describe this superb novel adequately, but it can be said that it is written in an experimental style resembling that of the early Dos Passos and the style of the Nighttown scene in ULYSSES. It was originally published in Paris more than thirty years ago, and it has been called every-

thing from "a great comic adventure" to "the first surrealist novel in English." Completely revised for this edition by Mr. Coates, it contains an introduction by him giving in detail the circumstances of its composition and his intentions in writing it. *A Putnam Capricorn Original.* 128 pp. $.95.

19a, and 19b. *James Viscount Bryce*, THE AMERICAN COMMONWEALTH. Completely edited, abridged and introduced by Louis Hacker, Professor of Economics, Columbia University, and former Dean of the School of General Studies. A completely new edition of this great work on the American system of government. Always mentioned in the same breath with De Tocqueville's earlier work, Lord Bryce's superb study of the American commonwealth has been edited for Capricorn by a distinguished American scholar and historian for the present age. *A Putnam Capricorn Original.* 2 vols. $1.35 each (Hardcover, 1 vol. $5.00).

20. *George Moore*, CONFESSIONS OF A YOUNG MAN, A famous book by a most unusual man, this memoir concerns Moore's life in the Paris of the Nineties, when he lived a rich and crowded existence in his apartment in the *Rue de la Tours des Dames* (an unusually appropriate name), "with all its charming adjuncts, palms and pastels, my cat, my python, my friends, blonde hair and dark." It also details Moore's friendships with the Decadent and Symbolist writers, and with Manet, Degas and Renoir. This account sums up the artistic life of the Nineteenth Century, and was a prime influence on Ezra Pound, T. S. Eliot and James Joyce. 288 pp. $1.25.

OTHER CAPRICORN BOOKS

1. *John Dewey*, ART AS EXPERIENCE. 384 pp. $1.35.

2. *Rainer Maria Rilke*, NOTEBOOKS OF MALTE LAURIDS BRIGGE. 256 pp. $1.15.

3. *Alfred Adler*, WHAT LIFE SHOULD MEAN TO YOU. 320 pp. $1.25.

4. *Clive Bell*, ART. 192 pp. $1.25.

5. *Alfred North Whitehead*, MODES OF THOUGHT. 256 pp. $1.15.

6. *Henry Adams*, DEGRADATION OF THE DEMOCRATIC DOGMA. With an Introduction by Brooks Adams. 320 pp. $1.25.

7. *Frederick Law Olmsted*, THE SLAVE STATES (BEFORE THE CIVIL WAR). Edited, with an Introduction, by Harvey Wish, author of SOCIETY AND THOUGHT IN AMERICA. 256 pp. $1.25 (Hardcover $2.50).

8. THE AUTOBIOGRAPHY OF THOMAS JEFFERSON. With an Introduction by Dumas Malone. 128. pp. $.95 (Hardcover $2.50).

9. NEWS AND RUMOUR IN RENAISSANCE EUROPE — THE FUGGER NEWSLETTERS. Edited by George T. Matthews. 256 pp. $1.25 (Hardcover $2.50).

10. *Graham Hough*, THE DARK SUN: A STUDY OF D. H. LAWRENCE. 272 pp. $1.25.

11. COLERIDGE'S WRITINGS ON SHAKESPEARE. Edited by Terence Hawkes. With an Introduction by Alfred Harbage. 256 pp. $1.35. (Hardcover $2.50).

12. *George Bernard Shaw*, THE ADVENTURES OF THE BLACK GIRL IN HER SEARCH FOR GOD. Illustrations by John Farleigh. 98 pp. $.95. (Hardcover $2.50).

13. *Alfred North Whitehead*, SYMBOLISM. 98 pp. $.95.

14. *William Golding*, LORD OF THE FLIES. With a biographical and critical note by E. L. Epstein. 256 pp. $1.25.

G. P. PUTNAM'S SONS

210 Madison Avenue • New York 16, N. Y.

4560